SUNDOWNERS

VAMPIRES ARE ONLY HUMAN

By Jeffrey V. Yorio

Cover by Juan Padron @ juanjpadron.com
Editing by Bambi Sommers

Special thanks to:

To my wife, Shaun, and daughter, Tempest, thanks for listening, helping, and not killing me.

To Court Ellyn for her encouraging words and great suggestions with a developmental edit and patience with my questions. Her Falcon series is well worth reading.

To Brian Fatah Steele for his support in getting my story off the ground. My notes to him may well have been as scary as any horror book he's written, do yourself a favor and check them out.

To my friends at the old Legend Fire writers' group, you all made me a better person and writer, thanks.

My Beta readers, Joan Daley, Geoff Ryder, Holly Rosalyn Kubasai, Nancy Moors, Alice Lombardo, and Steven Streeter.

Lastly but by no means least, to Bambi Sommers for her editing skill and patience on getting my first book to the finish line, thank you.

PROLOGUE

Poenari Castle, Wallachia, Romania.

The last of the guards, a cousin named Pitor, slumped to the ground, his head twisted one hundred and eighty degrees. She barely glanced at the body as she opened the double doors and looked at her quarry sitting on a throne.

"Dear uncle, you thought family would deter me from my mission, you should've stayed dead. You created a really good death; it was ninety-nine percent believable." Henriette said.

"I had my hopes, dear niece. If I may ask, where did I go wrong?"

"Allowing your brother to have your castle. The Turk might have given it to him, you'd have burned it down to prevent that. I do like what you've done to the place. Bats, wolves, gargoyles, and sulfur infused torches."

"Join me! We'll rule the world."

"Your side tried that, and humans called it the hundred year's war. Our kind was devastated. It'll be centuries, maybe a millennium, to recover. Does death enchant you so much?"

"The result justifies the method."

"Your cousin would hate you for corrupting his words. The Dongoj de Morto (Fangs of Death) has consumed you. Humans can't learn of this…of us."

"They already suspect and as you are my niece, you'll suffer this in due time, Henriette. Why not join me now, instead of waiting for it to take you?"

"I'm not evil or a monster like you. Tonight, Vlad Dracula, of clan Draculesti, the Impaler, dies."

"Then come and enter the Draco Vydra with me and we'll see if your words are prophetic."

CHAPTER 1

Ashland, Ohio

Agate watched the brick and slate Cape Cod from some bushes on the side of the house. The gabled eaves, styled shutters, gray brick walls, and second story back deck. Oh, what a facade you created, you evil son of a bitch.

The front door opened. Three women carrying cleaning supplies left saying thank you to a man with a beard: Mike Dunbar. The women climbed into a van decorated in bold print: "The Minute Maids. Always glad to squeeze you in." As they drove away, Mike closed the door. Agate checked her watch, 5:15pm.

In over four hundred years, I've killed, stolen, lied and a host of other things I'm not proud of. I've never killed for pleasure! You call it hunting. Now, you're the hunted.

The garage door opened and a Ford Transit with a luggage carrier, pulled out. Mike Dunbar leaving on his annual camping and trapping expedition at the nearby Funk Bottom Wildlife Area. Agate looked at the approaching dark sky and smiled. Large raindrops started falling about an hour later. Shakespeare ain't got nothing on the tempest I'll be!

Agate waited to see if the approaching storm changed Mike's plans. It didn't. The young trees that lined the street to Dunbar's house, bent to the wind. A garbage can tumbled past, subject to the errant gusts. Then the deluge came. Noah would've have felt at home. Neither rain nor wind mattered to Agate. She ignored the discomfort of her silver streaked, chestnut hair, as it matted to her neck. The water trickled into her London Fog trench coat. Agate strode to a tall pine tree in Mike's backyard, her Harley Davidson boots squishing through the water-soaked ground. She leaned against the tree's trunk and started pushing, her heart beating faster, her breathing becoming heavier, as she continued to push. She laughed upon feeling the sting of sweat run into her eye, amid the driving rain. Her boots made small furrows in the soaked ground, yet she was rewarded for her effort; the base of the pine tree moved. Its roots loosened and the surrounding dirt gathered in clumps away from the base, making it easier to move. A strong gust almost caused her to slip. Agate grabbed a low branch to steady herself. With a powerful shove, the wet ground finally lost its hold and roots began breaking as they emerged from the ground. The tree toppled onto the deck; the sound of breaking glass heard over the boom from a nearby lightning bolt.

Hope you don't have a cut-rate insurance company. Agate smirked and with the grace of a panther, jumped onto the tree trunk. Mike, you're a pathetic excuse for a vampire. She stepped through the branches and on to the deck, crunching broken glass beneath her boots. I'd never let a wet behind the ears piece of shit like you bring me to your version of hell! I saw that Jubilea Simbolo pin at last year's alumni dinner. You Traditionalists are twisted and evil, the worst traits of vampires and humans. Your fellow Traditionalists killed my mother and caused my daughter immense pain. Now I get to return some of that, in kind.

Just you and one other remain to be dealt with. I'm still in control. The Fangs of Death haven't taken hold of me, yet. Then, I need to do what should have been done over one hundred and twenty years ago.

Agate closed her eyes remembering a time over a century ago. The scene around her changed from the tree damaged deck. She was now in her bedroom, just a few blocks in distance yet many years in time and location, away from here. A young lady on a rose topped, four poster bed was giving birth. The sounds and smells of bread sellers and fish mongers, in French, were heard outside.

"That's good, Talrya, push, push. Yes, I seen the crown."

"Help! Mother, the pain, it's so much." Talrya lay there, legs spread, her body bathed in sweat.

"One more big push should do it, dear."

"I hate you, Armin Vanbery!" Talrya screamed as she provided the push her mother asked for.

"I hope you and Bram have fun in hell!"

"Oh, Talrya, Armin will pay for what he did. I promise that my erstwhile brother's days are numbered. As for the baby, it's a boy and looks healthy as well. Why, he even has split eyes, one hazel and the other blue."

"Bram and Armin can never know, never! Armin's as deranged as Uncle Vlad was."

"Yes dear, I'll see that they don't. I can take care of Bram as well if you'd like. Now, I'll clean the baby up and then you can hold him. Have you thought of a name?"

"I don't want to hold it or name it. I told you to kill it. It's an abomination!"

"It's a baby, Talyra, your son. It didn't get to pick its parents. Yet, it's your child, so as you wish. According to our custom."

Should I have killed the boy as Talyra wished, and not given him to a troupe of gypsy vampires who owed me a favor or made her keep the baby to raise? It turns out that showing mercy to that baby was a mistake that's been seeking me for well on thirty years now. Well, Bram and Armin did get theirs.

Some larger pieces of glass clung to the door frame and these she knocked in. A jagged corner nicked her left wrist. Blood oozed from the small cut and Agate felt the craving inside her growing. NO! I'll not give into you! I still control my body! The Dongoj de Morto will not control me. Her mind was on fire. Her body needed blood, desired blood, and craved blood. She began to feel pain in her jaws. She clenched her left fist and slammed it into the palm of her right hand and focused on a pleasant memory from her past. Her eidetic memory playing another movie.

She was in a meadow outside of Parma in late spring with her lover and remembered the words he told her.

"They who believe that you are incapable of making a man equally happy all the twenty-four hours of the day have never known you, Henriette. The joy which floods my soul is far greater when I converse with you during the day than when I hold you in my arms at night. Having read a great deal and having natural taste, you, Henriette, judge rightly of everything." A few tears began their slow trip down her cheek. Thank you, my dearest Giacomo!

The blood craving, or Fangs of Death, subsided for now. This was the curse of all vampires, that in their old age, they could go feral or lose control when they saw or smelled blood. That's what happened to her uncle and she killed him to protect the vampire existence. Agate entered the room and headed for the security panel. She entered the code and waited.

One of my students wanted a letter of recommendation for graduate school. I asked for a security code for one of her dad's clients. The all-clear green light blinked and then the phone rang. She picked it up and then put her vocal skill to use.

"Mr. Dunbar, this is Nova Home Security. Is everything all right?"

"Yes," Agate said in a male voice. "A tree in my back yard was toppled by the high winds and broke a sliding door, that's all. I'll call my insurance company in the morning," Agate said.

"Okay, Mr. Dunbar, voice analysis is confirmed, have a good evening."

"Thank you, sir, and I hope you have a good evening as well." Agate said, smiling as she replaced the phone on its wall mount, leaving the security system off.

Now, where would that cockroach of a worm keep a list? She looked about the bedroom. Well, your taste in paintings is dubious, Monet, Renoir and Sorolla. Agate picked up a pen from the nightstand and moved the pictures, nothing behind them. Then she went to the bookcase. Among the books were copies of Polidori's The Vampyre, Shelly's Frankenstein and Stoker's Dracula. Stoker was an idiot and a hack; well the hack part is my opinion!

She took Frankenstein off the shelf that had a piece of paper as a bookmark. Well, well, Mike. It appears even we are creatures of habit. You work in records and couldn't resist keeping a record of your contact's name, cities, and job. In a book about creating a better man is a list of people who want to create a better vampire. Only one more name.

She spent several minutes reading the information of the one name she needed. replaced the list and slid the book neatly back on the shelf, where it had come from.

Knowing what kind of filth, you are, I used some of my grandson's company's equipment to monitor your phone. You told Fortesque that you had found a vampire, that was a bad idea, and you were looking into the possibility that other vampires were in this area, a dumb idea. Now that I've got the name I wanted, I'll change a few of the paintings in my house. I know you have the pictures the police took in my house. If my time allows, I can correct for the mercy I should never have shown. Humans have this thing they call a bucket list. Things to do before they die. I never understood why this was important to many of them. But now I know it's because they don't have enough time and I appreciate that.

Funk Bottoms

Funk Bottoms Wildlife Area. A fancy name for a wannabe swamp and location used for fraternity hazing events. The home to birds, beavers, otters, foxes, and fish, along with the predators that feed on them. Mike never bothered them, and they could tell not to bother him. There's a reason he had a coyote pelt on the wall in his basement.

Mike Dunbar enjoyed his annual camping trip here. His traps had all been checked and reset and he was cooking dinner over the campfire as he waited for Laurent Fortesque, the Chief Editor of Al-Jazeera America and number three vampire in America. It made a good location to avoid any chance of observation. Though Mike doubted if more than fifty people in Ashland knew what Al-Jazeera was, not to mention Laurent. Laurent loved his power, used his power, and craved more. Not doing what he requested of you was close to questioning his power. It could earn you a broken bone, so Mike had heard. He turned to better thoughts. He knew the storm was coming and had set his traps up two days ago. Being a few weeks after season wasn't a concern; he'd paid for the privilege. Several good beaver pelts, two red fox, a nice gray, three muskrat and a raccoon, not a bad catch at all. The storm had only brought rain and wind, but after he'd set up camp.

The nighttime noises of owls, crickets, bull frogs, and a coyote didn't bother him. They were all part of the scenery like the tall reeds and cottontails swaying in the light wind and the wispy clouds in the starry night sky. He chuckled at the old movies where wolves, bats, and dogs could recognize his kind and even to some extent be controlled by us. That was a nice included fiction to our story, even if it created a misunderstanding about wolves and bats.

The savory smell of fish with garlic, blood sausages, and stuffed peppers, made his mouth water. He removed the cover to check how they were doing. Almost ready, a few more minutes. He reached down and brought up a pepper mill, grinding some onto the fish.

"Thank you, San Guine Pharmaceuticals. You make the best ground blood meal pellets, especially those flavored with cayenne pepper and cinnamon."

He'd brought the envelope containing Agate's missing persons file along with his personal file on Agate. Why Laurent wanted it made no sense. It had cost him a few favors and several thousand bucks, but Laurent had promised to cover any expenses he incurred.

As the assistant director of Records and Transcripts at Ashland University, he had access to student and teacher data, it was by accident that he discovered that Agate was a vampire.

People never stop doing what they like. Agate was head of the Universities Art and Humanities Department, some of her vases were on display in the foyer. Oh, he'd seen her picture hanging on the wall for years, but it was her French style pottery that made the connection. Despite our long lives and good memories, there was no way vampires could tell one of theirs from a human. I remember my lessons in Esperanto in Warsaw. God, I hated that teacher...Mrs. Steinhowski. I lost track at one hundred, the number of times she rapped my hand for not knowing. We have a language very few others know. Agate had been able to hide right under his nose for almost fifteen years. Her new ID was amazing, professional work. It had taken him over a year of hard exhaustive computer detective work, to find that it was fake. That was why he contacted Laurent. Laurent wanted information about old European vampires.

Somehow, she'd learned about his searches, he had no clue how or why, but she'd run.

He checked her accounts, no activity after several thousand-dollar withdrawals. A few days later, a one-way ticket to Paris, leaving from Cincinnati under the name of Agatha DiStangio.

How easy was that. He filed an anonymous missing person's report.

The police searched her house, taking pictures of every room. They checked her computer and voice messages. There was no sign of a struggle. The report had listed several calls from Sofia, Bulgaria, where her daughter lived, along with many calls from students and fellow teachers.

All the pictures, original report, and transcripts of the phone calls, he'd placed in three envelopes. Yet, her existence here made him think that there were more vampires. That was the reason for Laurent. He'd called him back and asked, "Are there anymore?" He had assured Laurent that he was looking into that possibility. Checking records to see who may have moved into this area within a six-month period of Agate's arrival. Name changes and death records of newborns, to see if any new social security numbers had been issued. Mike looked at the full moon, a Blood Red Hunters Moon, poetic looking out from behind a few wispy clouds. We are the next step in evolution, just as humans supplanted primates.

Mike heard a splash from the water and stood up. "Such an amateur, using a paddle like that."

"Is that you, Mike Dunbar?" a voice called.

"Yes, who are you?"

"I'm Laurent Fortesque."

"Mr. Fortesque, please come on up. I hope you didn't have too much trouble finding me?"

"No problem at all, your directions were very good."

He saw Laurent bringing his canoe toward his little island camp. He barely knows how to paddle and isn't sitting in the middle of the canoe. He's an amateur. Laurent beached his canoe and almost fell into the water, as he got out.

"Good evening, Mr. Dunbar. Sorry for the unusual meeting place. But just wanted to eliminate any unforeseen circumstances. I hope you're trapping has been going well."

"It has, Mr. Fortesque, thanks for asking."

"You're welcome, did you bring what I asked?"

"Yes, sir, it's in my tent."

He looks different, shorter than I expected.

"Mike, I appreciate your timely work." The voice changed from male to female as the figure was now close enough for Mike to see it clearly in the campfire's light. It wasn't Laurent Fortesque. It was Agate D'Estange.

Mike's eyes widened, his face began to perspire, his hands clenched and unclenched rapidly. "You're supposed to be in Paris!" he spurted. "You ran. I figured that we'd have to hunt you down. Well, I must admit, that voice trick is rare, and you had me fooled but you'll not be able to tell anyone, you French bitch."

Mike moved away from the campfire, and a little closer to Agate. He crossed his arms such that his right palm was on his left shoulder and his left was on his right shoulder. He then bowed and spread his arms out, to the side, open palms toward Agate, to show he had no weapons. Agate returned the gesture. The Draco Vydra challenge. For over two thousand years, the only way vampires would fight each other. All vampire clans, princedoms and regions ran tournaments. Now such was the only peaceful gathering between the two factions.

"So, Draco Vydra then," said Agate.

"I'd not have you think that we Traditionalists don't value our traditions."

"Torture isn't a tradition. Murder isn't a justifiable behavior; genocide isn't either, but that's what you are doing. Besides, run away from the likes of you, Mike? Hardly!" she covered her mouth while laughing and slowly moving closer.

"But you thought so, didn't you? I purchased a ticket with the money I withdrew, for a friend of mine, and your imagination ran with it. You're so used to trapping and hunting, you've no idea what it's like to be on the receiving end. The fact that you could be hunted just isn't something you believe could happen."

Agate was now about ten feet from him.

"That's irrelevant, soon you'll be at our research facility. All that matters is how much pain I inflict before you're defeated." Mike took up a Draco Vydra defensive position.

Agate slightly shook her head at Mike's pose. I thought he was a champion, not a child.

"Oh, Wyvern's defense, not a bad choice, but not a good one either." Agate replied as she leaped at him, her foot aiming for his stomach.

Mike twisted to avoid the leg, realizing the deception, and blocked her from slashing his throat.

Agate landed on the edge of the tent, in a crouching position. Mike moved in, Naga attack, as his fingers attempted to stab Agate's neck.

"Oh, Mikey, Mikey, you aren't better than I thought, your tournament victories led me to think you were good."

"What do you mean, bitch?"

Agate launched into a whirlwind attack with her arms, she was fast, yet Mike blocked them. The sound of bone breaking, brought a chuckle from Agate. Mike felt the pain radiate up his arm, like nothing he'd experienced before.

"I'll make you pay for that." His left arm had a trickle of blood where the bone had almost broken the skin. Sweat was coming down his face, his eyes filled with rage.

"Well, if that's really how you want it, that's fine with me." The contempt in her voice was very evident. "You see Mike, like all good hunters, I studied my prey before I went hunting. I never knew until now, how exhilarating, relaxing and downright enjoyable hunting is."

"Hunting, you're about to get a free lesson in hunting." Mike attacked; his leg swipe caused Agate to lose her balance as his fist slammed into her side. He knew he'd hurt her, yet his smile didn't last long as her left hand gripped his.

She brought her leg up into his left leg, and again the sound of bone breaking resounded. Mike fell to the ground, winced, and cursed in pain. Agate grabbed Mike and tossed him into the campfire. Mike rolled off and stood up, but his expression gave away his thoughts; he was a goner.

Mike was doing his best to defend from the bitch's attacks but with a broken leg and arm, he had few options. He was able to land blows, but he always took one for each one he landed. His breathing was heavier, harder. He was sweating profusely. There was no escape route.

"Well Mike, how does it feel to be hunted? How does pain feel? You Traditionalists killed my mother, Dolcinea. You use torture for a science experiment, all to produce a better vampire."

"Killing me won't change that."

"That's why I want you alive. You'll give me all the information I desire and then your death will be as slow as I can make it. I'm not sure if I hope to enjoy torturing you. I don't want to become you, but sometimes you need to get down in the mud with monsters to remove them."

"Listen, you French bitch. Once we've captured you, we'll get that pimp grandson of yours next."

Agate's eyes widened. "Never!" She screamed as her fists smashed into Mike's face, hammering his nose. Then she picked him up and tossed him into the rack that held his animal furs. Mike saw something in her eyes, the snarl of her lips. Her open mouth revealing fangs. She started to think of her one love, Giacomo, but the craving came on too fast and too strong. She felt the pain of her fangs growing. She looked down at Mike's almost unconscious body, blood oozing out of his smashed nose, split upper lip and a mouth missing a few teeth.

"That's it, you whore, kill me and be done with it." As he spat at her.

"So hard not to, the blood calls to me."

"Feast on his blood! They want Prince Tepes, then give it to them! They killed me most foul, daughter," said her mother, Dolcinea.

"No, my dearest Henriette, you need him alive," said the voice of Giacomo, in her head.

"The craving is too much. He dies as I feast."

The last thing Mike saw was Agate's open mouth and fangs, descending toward him. His scream became a gurgle. She removed a mouthful of neck which she spat on the ground, drinking the blood that flowed from the opening. The craving decreased, replaced by a euphoric feeling, like a junkie who'd taken their fix. And soon, the control of her mind was hers again.

Shit! I don't remember killing him, nor wanting to! That's what happens, no memory of what you do during the craving. This changes my plans. Not as much time left as I thought. What do Americans say? It is what it is. Need to make the best of it. At least I considered this possibility.

She cleaned her face at the water's edge and retrieved a change of clothes from the canoe. The blood-stained clothes she burned in the campfire. She carried Mike's body to the shore placing it at the edge of the water. Then she tied a rope around it and pulled it to a little hillock, several hundred feet away.

She placed Mike's left foot in a small trap, it snapped with a resounding clank.

"Checking your traps at night is dangerous, Mr. Dunbar, at least you won't be able to gnaw your foot off and get away."

Now back to the tent and that package, then a quick trip home to take care of a few things.

CHAPTER 2

Venice, Italy

Zephrin was in his workshop, constructing a glass unicorn. I'll give it a blue horn, he decided, as he finished attaching a green tail. It already had a yellow mane and red flaming hooves.

"I'll call you Zephyr's Harbinger."

At the same time, he was thinking, Harlison Darneys doesn't know the difference between a hobby and a passion. It escapes him.

 Glass, be it stained, Murano, or other, was his passion. Zephrin was the chief special operative for I.S.I.A. or International Security Investigation Agency. He was the owner, but he kept that well-hidden. Zephrin preferred the field over the board room. Being over one hundred and ten years old and with a special memory, his talent was figuring out crimes and mysteries.

He detached Zephyr's Harbinger from its glass handle and carried it to a large curio cabinet.

It contained several pieces, Excalibur by Steuben, some uranium glass, he was careful with that, knowing what radiation did to Marie Curie. There were some Chinese Panda Glass, Murano, Empoli and Victorian pieces. One shelf held paperweights and a third had fish, dragons, and other animals, now joined by a unicorn. He had no idea what they were worth, nor did he care. His insurance did care, and had a value for them, determined by two auditors.

He walked to a small counter to pick up a large manila envelope with his financial report inside and grabbed a blood orange.

His next stop was the fireplace, where he tossed the report. He watched it burn while peeling and eating the orange.

"A passion doesn't care about costs, Mr. Darneys. It's about love, not relaxation."

He walked to the window that presented him with an amazing view of Venice. The sun was now above the horizon. How glad I am that we aren't the creature of our own invention. I'd die at never being able to experience a beautiful sunrise or romantic sunset. Though a good sunscreen would be advisable. Of all the myths we created about ourselves, that's the one human's most associate with us. They put it into movies, books, and games. It was all a proof of the phrase; necessity is the mother of invention. For us vampires to survive, we created a myth based on a vampire affliction, our craving for blood, in the language of vampires, we call it 'Dongoj de Morto' or the 'Fangs of Death.' Oh yes, up to five hundred years ago it happened at a much higher frequency, now it was much rarer, perhaps one in ten of what it was in the past. That's why there are people like me, hunters, whose job is to put the afflicted out of their misery and protect the truth of our existence. Our idea: no secret can remain a secret, so we wanted to scare humans with something so frightening that they'd never believe it.

The Grand Canal was filled with gondolas and the Rialto was crowded with shoppers. In Italian he said,

"Gina, are you listening?"

His computerized personal assistant was patterned after Gina Lollobrigida. He smiled as he remembered meeting her in late 1947, and how he fell madly and passionately in love with her. For that reason, he chose to leave her and had to tell her why. He remembered the look on her face when he told her about himself. His mind started flipping through scenes.

It was Easter weekend, 1948. They were at La Rocca Abbaziale de Subiaco. The sunlight coming through the window caused her eyes to sparkle as it played on her face. He brushed the hair off her forehead, then kissed it.

"Good morning, Gina."

"You said that an hour ago. Did you forget?"

"No, my love, you are a very distracting lady."

"Gina enjoys how you wake Gina up. Gina also likes making sure all your body is up as well."

"My love, I need to tell why I can no longer be with you."

Her eyes became a little larger and a scared look developed on her face.

"My love, Gina, I'm a vampire and yes, I know that sounds crazy."

"Zephy makes fun of Gina, Zephy not a vampire."

"Why would I tell you this if it weren't true?"

"Gina does not know, unless you have other lover, prettier than Gina."

"There is no lady on Earth prettier than you."

Gina sat up, the sheet spilling to her lap. She took one of his hands and placed it over her heart. She placed one of hers over his.

"Listen and feel how my heart speaks it's love for you. Yours is saying the same to me, Zephy. Gina doesn't care if you think you're a vampire."

"Gina, the pain I would have watching you grow old, would be the same as the pain you'd have watching me stay young."

"Zephy, love conquers all things, even time. How many people find true love? When you find such a treasure, you keep it. Gina doesn't care if you're a vampire.

So, what if Zephy stays young while Gina gets old? We'd still be together, that's what love is. Zephy, believe in me, like I believe in you. We love each other."

"Those are beautiful words, Gina. They almost make me believe but, Gina, love doesn't conquer time. Wherever you go or whatever you do, I'll love you. If you ever need anything, let me know and I'll do what I can to help."

"Gina will always love you and remember you. Zephy needs to learn why you don't use all of your heart, like your heart uses all of its chambers."

Her projection appeared on the wall, in a red dress with green trim speaking with her voice. Maybe you were right after all, dear.

"Yes, Zephrin, Gina is here; always ready to answer your beck and call. Now, what would you have of Gina?"

"Gina, why do you always appear in that dress?"

"Why, to remind you of your destructive nature towards clothes. I could appear wearing nothing if you wanted but, at your age, that might be dangerous."

Zephrin chuckled at her comment.

"Gina, please see that Mr. Darneys is paid his proper fee and then cancel him as my personal financial adviser and hire Deliotte, SPA of Rome, to replace him."

"Gina will see to it, dear. Is there anything else?"

"As I remember, I've no meetings or other important items to sink my teeth into."

"That's correct, Zephy is only left with idle imagination and obsessing."

"For dinner tonight, I'll have moussaka and liver tartar with a medium spicy blood sauce, and salad with Russian dressing. To drink, an Italian semi dry red cinzanno and for dessert, a pistachio Halva with blood pudding."

"Very good choices, Zephrin, Gina will place the order for 7pm."

"Were there any calls while I was… obsessing?"

"Your mother called and said to please call her back, as soon as you can."

"Do so now on speaker, it's unusual for mom to ask me to call back. Ciao, Gina."

"Ciao, dear," Gina said as she vanished. The phone rang twice.

"Oh Zephy, I'm so glad you called back," his mom said.

"What's up, Mom, is something wrong? Have you and Dad split up again, or is it gotten back together? I can't remember which it would be now."

"Why, we're still together, so far... Zephy, this is serious. I haven't heard from Agate in over two weeks. The last time we talked she was distracted, repeated herself and talked about missing her little Prince. Then she mentioned a craving for some new blood in her life."

"Mom, Grandma's probably gallivanting around France right now, with some lucky young man. I don't see anything to worry about."

"Zephy, you do need to be more aware of your family. That business of yours is taking you away from matters of the family and clan. Agate has been living in America for about fifteen years now."

"Really?! I thought that was a vacation or a conference she was at. She actually sold her little Parisian cottage and moved to America?"

"No dear, she moved, but she paid for her cottage to be disassembled, shipped and reassembled in America. You do remember how she loved that cottage."

"Yes. I can't believe she'd do that. I wonder what's gotten into her."

He'd spent a lot of time there as a kid helping her paint, cook, learned the basics of pottery, didn't learn the basics of painting, and worked in her flower garden. She taught him her job as a hunter, to replace her.

"Well, to America, I'll go check in on her. Will it be to New York, Las Vegas or Los Angeles?"

"Zephrin, you're still not listening to me. I fear that Agate is developing the Fangs of Death. You'll need to travel to Ashland, Ohio and the university there where she works."

That idiot Stoker immortalized the Dongoj de Morto or Fangs of Death with his book. We used that to make humans fear us, the fact that some older vampires went feral, giving into the call of blood. A disease to some, curse to others, it was to scare, frighten and sicken those who read or heard about us.

Zephrin paused before continuing, knowing what was coming.

"I've never heard of Ashland, Ohio."

"Well, you do own an international detective agency; use it. I'm hiring ISIA to check in on her. Please, Zephy, I'm scared for her. She called you her little Prince for a reason. Please call me when you know something."

"I'll leave in the morning, Mom."

"Thank you, dear. It's the way she'd want it to be and even if you weren't, I'd still call you a prince."

"Thanks, Mom, I'll call when I know what's up." A click ended the call.

Zephrin got up off the couch, walked over to the counter and picked up a blood orange and tossed it in the air a few times. Then he hurled it through the glass door to the balcony.

"Gina, please make arrangements for me to fly to the largest city nearest to Ashland, Ohio. I'll depart at 4am. Load a file to my computer about Ashland, the university, and any public references to Agate d'Estaing. Check on any strange deaths, missing persons or thefts and include a list of contacts in Ohio. Please see that a case of my personal beef jerky is on board and get the glass door fixed. Where will I be flying into, Gina?"

"Cleveland Hopkins International Airport. From there, you'll rent a car and take US 71 south to US 250 west into Ashland, estimated drive time is forty-five minutes. Gina will make all the arrangements. Would you like to book a room in Cleveland or Ashland?"

"Really, Gina, like you'd choose Ashland over Cleveland. A hotel near the airport, make it a suite. If I really need to get a room in Ashland, I will."

"Gina would take the location that was best for the purpose Gina was traveling to Ashland for, dear."

"Well, you're just a carry on, dear. Did I.T. finish the upgrade to my laptop?"

"Yes, they did, you now have full link-share capability with the Gina mainframe."

While over the Atlantic, Zephrin confirmed his bureaucratic papers. Copies of his ISIA, his Italian driver's license and I.D.P. His active status as a colonel in the Italian Carabinieri. Confirmation had been received from the U.S. State Department along with the Italian and Bulgarian Embassy's. He had declared his permits for his Beretta 8045F Cougar pistols. The U.S. Department of State had been contacted via Bulgaria's UN Ambassador about his arrival to investigate a missing person report of a Bulgarian national. He read the files while in flight. Agate moved to Ashland sixteen years ago, having accepted a job as professor of Art History at the University. There was a newspaper article about her cottage being disassembled, transported, and reassembled in Ashland.

It took a year. Four years later she became head of the Art History and Humanities department. He noticed a police report. An anonymous caller had filed a missing person report fourteen days ago. There was no information in the report. That bothered him, reports should help answer questions not create more.

As of last night, no other missing person reports had been filed in the Ashland area. No murders and only two break-ins associated with a recent storm. Police had already arrested suspects for one of the break-ins.

The file about Agate included information from Ashland University. Her bio for the college noted that Agate had been an associate professor at Sorbonne, Paris. It included her picture along with images of some of her paintings and pottery. He smiled, recognizing the painting. Her farm and apple orchard at the cottage. It was outside of Paris; several little boys ran between the apple trees. All were of him; she'd just painted him doing different things.

Okay Baba, why did you leave Paris? Like a maze, I see no path, no reason, so what would cause you to move to Ashland, Ohio and bring your cottage with you?

He perused the contacts file. Closing his eyes, he shook his head, it wasn't as good as it could be. He had three contacts in Cleveland, one in a place called Wooster, and three more in the state capital of Columbus. It took but a few minutes for him to remember their names and send a contact message about his arrival.

Next, he saw the name Laurent Fortesque, the number three vampire in America and director of Al-Jazeera America, an extremely dangerous vampire, probably as good as Zephrin in Draco Vydra, and a hunter of vampires affected with the Fangs of Death. They hated but respected each other. He was the enemy, or as close as vampires could be since both the Princes Council and American Vampire Council had denied all requests for war. Laurent was a Traditionalist, or as most vampires called them, Dracula cultists, they wanted to become Dracula. They wanted to take the wild animal, the diseased creature that Vlad Tepes had become and give that to all vampires. The power and strength of affected vampires was not to be denied. Yet, such was craziness. The study to develop a cure, would be a worthwhile goal, but they didn't do research for a cure, they did research to isolate its causes. His father, Sebastian Cole, had argued before the joint councils and shown evidence of their testing on humans.

Sebastian and Zephrin had found one of their research facilities. Dr. Moreau had designed the labs used in that South American facility. Human babies, young children, and elderly, all showing signs of affliction. They were locked in cages or chained to the walls. There were bodies on examination tables with their brains exposed and jaws in sections. He remembered many of them begging to be killed, telling stories of being injected and then having a craving overtake them. Stories of then killing their children, wife, or siblings that had been locked in with them. It was at some place in Guyana, maybe forty years ago. Those pictures had reviled the joint council. However, they had no documented proof of testing being done on vampires. Nor was there anything that even hinted at a connection to or with Laurent. None of the vampires found were born as vampires. They were experimental humans, a result of an injection of the blood from an infected vampire and they were dying. Supposition and conjecture but nothing conclusive, so they were left with their little Cold War.

The joint councils had ordered them to immediately stop all testing on humans. Then ordered the death of four vampires for such experimentation. At least Dr. Frankenstein used dead bodies for his work but even that had bad consequences.

We must keep our existence a secret. If we became known, the humans would wipe us out. Contrary to popular myth, we can be killed by guns and other weapons. It's the image we created of ourselves that needs a stake in the heart. Oh, a lot of humans would die. When you're fighting for your life, you'll do anything to win.

If Laurent knew Agate was missing or that Zephrin was on his way to look for her, then the hunt would be on, and for Agate's sake, he had to win that hunt. He reclined in the leather chair. He had time to rest now. Zephrin's subconscious grappled with what he knew.

He remembered many years ago. Agate asked him, "Zephy, why do you kill feral vampires?"

"Baba," he remembered saying, "They have to be. To protect the knowledge of our existence, to provide a painless and quick death, and to save the afflicted from the evil of being tortured." Zephrin's eyes closed as he thought about ending, as peacefully as possible, the pain that Agate was going through. His final thoughts before sleep overcame him were of Agate and how long it had been since he'd seen her and what her reply had been, "Zephy, murder is murder, it can't be justified." Where are you, Baba? Be safe, I'll find you soon.

CHAPTER 3

Ashland, Ohio

The fax machine chimed and, shortly after, a sheet of paper began crawling out. A man reached for it and, in the process, knocked his coffee mug over.

"Shit! Damn coffee always in the way. Hey, Chuck, we've got a flash fax that came in from both State and FBI," said Lt. Cecil Saunders, head of Ashland's detectives.

Chuck Tompkins was Chief of Police for the city of Ashland, Ohio, and local denizen of Ashland's schools.

"Bring it in, Cecil, and come sit. I had a call about this last night and I want to talk a few things over with you."

Cecil sat in the chair under the window while Chuck read the fax. There were two baseball bats, mounted on the wall, one from high school and the other from college. Chuck's desk was much neater than his but the floor by the waste basket showed why Cecil always won when they played hoops. "Is this about that international detective, who's coming to check on our missing professor?"

"Yes, it is, so my first question is, did you know that our missing persons file on Professor Agate d'Estange is empty? The pictures we took, are not in the evidence locker and the computer file is empty. I.T. is looking into it. I need to know what you remember about our missing professor that was in that file, Cecil. Next, the Bulgarian

UN Ambassador contacted the State Department about this investigator coming here."

"Someone has some clout. No, I didn't know the file was empty, as for Agate d'Estange, she's of dual citizenship, French and Bulgarian. She has one daughter who's married and lives in Sofia, Bulgaria. She'd been living in France for over thirty years, an associate professor at an art university there, when she took the job here. She had her house from France rebuilt here about a year later."

"Did you see anything unusual at her house?"

"Just the house, well a stone cottage, kind of like a Cape Cod house, otherwise nothing that wouldn't be in a typical older lady art professor's house. We took the standard pictures of all the rooms. It was a neat house, well cared for. There were three rooms on the second floor, a bedroom, bathroom, and studio, where she painted and made pottery. The house had paintings, country and farm scenes, hanging in most of the rooms, otherwise, nothing remarkable at all."

"Well, you're one hell of a detective. I don't believe in coincidences, so put that file back together ASAP. I want to know who would hire a detective to look for a missing person? Who would have the money to do that and why? What makes our missing professor so important and why our file is empty, though I.T. is handling that problem."

"Sure will, Chuck."

New York City

The secretary knocked on Laurent Fortesque's door, Director of Al-Jazeera America.

"Come in."

As she entered, the swarthy man at the desk, a hint of red in his hair and his devilishly unusual eyes, one hazel and the other blue, was working two cell phones and a computer. He looked up saying, in an aggravated tone "What do you need me for?"

"Mr. Fortesque, you said to let you know if our Ohio representative missed his deadline. Mr. Dunbar is now thirty-six hours overdue."

Laurent Fortesque told those on his cell phones that he'd get back to them and closed his laptop.

"Have we tried to reach him?"

"Yes, sir. We only get his answering machine at home and his cell phone goes right into message."

His lips pursed, his eyes narrowed, and he spoke in a soft, yet staccato manner.

"Rather unfortunate timing on his part. Okay, move another article into his slot and see that he isn't paid for work not delivered. Oh, and send Rachael in to see me."

"Yes, sir," she said as she left and closed the door.

Dunbar, Mike Dunbar. That name...ah, yes, we've spoken several times. His last call, he said that he might have found a vampire and was investigating. That was several months ago, maybe even a year.

Laurent pulled out his minicomputer and brought up Mike Dunbar's file:

Assistant Director of Records and Transcripts at Ashland University.

Avid trapper and camper.

Jubileo Simbolo member for forty-three years.

Eleven years at current position.

Called nine months ago about a possible vampire target at his University and was investigating. I called back five months ago and asked what he knew. A female professor at the University might be a vampire. Her background, Eastern European, was being investigated by his team. I told him to update me when he was 100% sure with his research.

Okay, let's see about this University. He entered Ashland University. The Ashbrook Center highly rated. Constitutional self-government, history, political science, and international studies.

Yes, I know why the name is familiar, Robin Meade graduated from there. Current enrollment of Muslim students is over one hundred, most in the Ashland Center for English Studies. I see an excellent article for Al-

Jazeera and, therefore, a reason for me to go to there and follow up about this vampire Mike found.

He put his minicomputer away as Rachael Ganam, his assistant editor, entered his office. She was Egyptian but had lived and studied in London for ten years. Brown eyes, black hair and one of the few attractive ladies who refused his charms and flirtations. She had a live-in boyfriend and was very loyal, a trait that Laurent respected and admired.

Rachael took the view of Leila Ahmed and felt that the society one lives in defines modesty. More proof that Americans are much more like Romans than they think. Pickers and choosers of culture, architecture, language from other cultures. Modern day raiders and pillagers. My, did they howl, when I hired her for this position. My response was I need those who can blend in, do a good job and help give and provide a different view of Islam and our faith. A few of my connections helped as well.

"Yes, Laurent, what's on your mind?"

"With all this about ISIS and America's preoccupation with Muslim extremists, we've covered the big cities, topics and subjects. Have we ever done mid-America, it's heart, stuff away from the big metropolitan areas?"

"Not exactly sure what you mean but in general, no, we don't cover small cities, not enough resources and no obvious reason. Why?"

"I'm going to do an article showing America what young American Muslims, in a small city, think about what's going on. About how non-Muslims and Muslims get along.

We'd be presenting an image that some Americans want to see. Show people that not all Muslim's are like their more fanatical brothers and sisters. The non-stereo types."

Rachael pursed her lips while looking at him.

"Yes, a story away from the big cities and bright lights. Could work but could fail. What location do you have in mind and who would do it?"

"A place called Ashland University in Ashland, Ohio. I was reading about it and it looks like a good place, over one hundred Muslim students in a rural area of a 'swing state.' As for who, well, me of course. It's been a while since I've done an article. I need to practice, and you're better than me at running this place, I just make outside decisions and sign the checks. You'll be fine for a few weeks."

"Okay, we'll do it as an Op-Ed piece. Up to five thousand words and get as many quotes as you can. Some pictures wouldn't hurt, either. Can you have it in, at most, six days and it'll run in the next issue? How will you get there, plane?"

"No, I'll drive. It'll let me see the land, get a feel for the people of that area. My car will be fine and yes, I'll keep all my receipts. Oh, and please make a reservation at Empellon for me. I'd best get in one good meal, before I hit the road in the morning."

"Okay then, Laurent, have a good trip and bring back a great article."

Thanks, Rachael, I'm sure I will."

Ashland, Ohio

Brielle Chalmers entered Agate's class and heard the sigh from the students. Her figure made fantasies about the weekend rather interesting and more film oriented than Romanticism art. Her medium brown skin, green eyes, and brown-red hair. She put her briefcase on the desk and began.

"I've heard from Professor d'Estange and she's in Sofia, dealing with the estate of her recently deceased sister. She's asked me to take over her class assignments for the rest of the semester. Since this was a sudden death, if any of you would like to send her a card, I'll see what I can do to get it to her. She said she misses you all but will never forgive any drop in effort because she's not here. So, let's continue where she left off. The Renaissance affected social, political, and economic systems in Europe. Today we'll talk about the following. How and why did art became an outlet for political dissent, social non-conformity but still attract wealthy patrons and established institutions of that time."

This isn't like Agate, to miss a class, oh I understand the reason, but she's never mentioned a sister to me before.

The students mooned but opened notebooks and made computers ready.

Cecil was on the computer, regathering information about Agate D'Estange. Okay, enough checking on ESPN about the Browns loss yesterday. He changed to the Ashland University web page.

"Professor Agate d'Estange. Mother was Dolcinea d'Estange, her father was Stefan Vanbery. Seems she kept her mom's family name. Children, a daughter, Talrya Nekos, interesting as to why her last name isn't after either mother or father. Head geologist at the Bulgarian firm of SeCo. Otherwise, nothing that isn't in her University application CV."

I find that suspicious, though I can see why the University didn't. "Why does she hire an international detective agency to investigate her mother who she hasn't heard from for a few weeks? Why the concern? Should I pull the phone records? Would a judge grant me that, for a missing person? Doubt it. Okay, let's check out SeCo."

The results came up, several pages worth. Dunn and Bradstreet first. SeCo, a Bulgarian mining conglomerate, they produce copper, gold, iron, steel, lead, zinc, and manganese. They bought an Italian company last year that makes fluorspar. They also produce some natural gas. An excellent credit rating, owner is Sebastian Cole II, positive cash flow, small amount of debt. Founded by Sebastian Nekos-Cole and Marcus Sandoft, in 1904. Well, there's the last name answer.

Upon the death of Marcus, in 1971, total ownership transferred to Sebastian Cole, died in 1981, son took over leadership. Married to Talrya Nekos in 1959, divorced in

1979, they remarried in 1984. Well, there's the political and financial connection. He printed out the D & B report then called the University's Art department and said that he wanted to talk to all staff, individually, in two hours. Then pulled up pictures of Agate and Talyra. Both looked young for their age and they did have that family resemblance. Another interesting thing, not many pictures of the three of them at all. Granted, I doubt that Sofia, Bulgaria is the hot spot of young attractive billionaires or fancy summer vacations.

CHAPTER 4

Ashland, Ohio

Zephrin, reached Ashland about 5:30pm and headed for the police station to check in, as a courtesy. He opened the outer door, entering the causeway, when an alarm sounded. The doors locked and two officers emerged from a door on the opposite side, their 9mm Glock's drawn.

"Hands in the air," they shouted.

Zephrin complied and as the inner door opened, one officer approached, yelling instructions.

"Turn around, slowly, place your hands behind your head, interlace your fingers and kneel, crossing your legs."

Zephrin did so and they used plastic restraining strips, instead of handcuffs. This raised his opinion of the police. Push button entry but no challenge or query about my visit at the door. Nice thought about a metal scanner. The glass is bullet proof. The officers are professional and well trained, for a small college town.

They searched him, removing both of his guns along with his billfold and ID's. Then he was taken to a holding room for about five minutes. Two men entered, one with two cups of coffee. The other cut his restraining straps, then left.

"I'm Chuck Thompkins, the chief of police in Ashland, and I offer you my apologies, Colonel." He placed a cup of coffee on the table, in front of Zephrin.

"Coffee is black, hope you don't mind. I hope you weren't mistreated or offended. The metal detector sounded as you entered, everything else was just precautionary procedure. I'd been informed that you would be arriving but didn't expect you for another day."

"Mistreated? No, in that your officers were most respectful. It was nice to see that procedures and caution are followed. Would've been nice if that information had been passed on to your men. Your officers were efficient and treated me well. Please, no need to call me colonel, Zephrin or Mr. Ivano will be fine. Twelve hours is a long flight, but I decided to get here ASAP and check in, as a courtesy, so I could proceed with my investigation by looking Ms. d'Estange's house over. Could I see or, even better, have a copy of the missing person report filed about Ms. Agate d'Estange?"

Chuck Thompkins' face turned redder as Zephrin continued with his dissertation.

"You've got some nerve. You dare come into my city, my department and think that you're that important because you've got diplomatic connections? You're the presumptive one. Probably haven't done a hard day's detective work in your life. Checking on rich ladies missing cats or stolen coffee makers, as they lounge by the pool."

Uh oh, bad choice, I got the host police chief pissed at me, not one of my better choices. I need to rectify that. "Captain Thompkins, my apologies. Any captain, who would so defend his men and department, is a good leader and one whose officers should be most proud of serving under. I did you a grave disservice. I owe you and your department an apology." as Zephrin extended his hand to Captain Thompkins.

"Okay, Mr. Ivano, I accept your apology." as he shook Zephrin's hand. "However, forgiving and forgetting are still undecided. As for seeing the report, that would be difficult. Our I.T. director explained to me that another officer accidentally deleted it. I've assigned my lead detective to rebuild the missing persons file on professor d'Estange."

"Well accidents do happen, Captain." The file was deleted!? You fool, that was no accident. How does your department do anything more difficult than writing parking tickets and breaking up rancorous frat parties? Have you ever heard of backing up your computer?

"If my papers are in order, can I have my weapons back and carry them on campus as I check into Ms. d'Estange disappearance, for my client, her daughter?"

"Yes, you can, all your paperwork is in order. They're outside on the counter. Please enjoy your time in Ashland and if you need anything, let me know, politely, if you can."

If I ever need anything from this department, then I need to consider if I have the Fangs of Death! You might be proof of the stereotype of coffee drinking and doughnut eating American policemen. I saw two boxes of them in your cafeteria. Oh, and this swill you brought me; it's only relationship to coffee is that it was hot.

"My thanks, Captain Thompkins that is most generous of you. My client has provided me with a copy of the house key. Is it considered a police scene?"

"No, it isn't. If you have a key, go ahead, I don't think an escort will be necessary. Please don't remove anything from the location, though you can take all the pictures you like."

"Thank you very much, Captain." Right! My client gave me permission and if I feel it's needed, I'll remove anything I want to.

***

It was early in the morning, after her battle where she killed Mike. The sun was close to peaking over the horizon. Agate checked to see if anyone was outside as she approached her cottage. She was glad that hers was not like the others, all single floor, aluminum siding with either a back deck or sunroom. Her cottage of stone with her workshop and bedroom on the second floor. A woman's home is also her castle. None of her neighbors were out, even Mr. Santori, who loved to work in his garden, showing off his chest and zucchini, as he flirted with her. She went up to a window and started pressing the stones under the ledge. She smiled as one moved and pressed harder until it stopped. She lifted the window up and squeezed through the tighter than expected open window to her small guest room.

Damn, I'm becoming fat. Agate went upstairs, turned on her shower on and removed her mud-covered clothes and boots. After she finished the shower, she went to her closet, dressed, then selected two sweaters and a pair of sneakers. Moving to her armoire, she selected some casual workout pants, underwear, and shirts.

She stuffed these in a military duffel bag along with the washcloth she used to clean up. The wet clothes and boots, she stuffed into a trash bag, which just fit in the military duffel bag.

She went downstairs and checked the refrigerator, to see what there was to eat.

She smiled. I see that my curator has been here, anything that could spoil has been removed. She went to the pantry and took out some crackers, peanut butter and opened a jar of homemade strawberry jam. She sat at the table to eat her feast along with a bottle of water, while she thought. Now, what to do next? Can't call anyone. Knowing my daughter, my little prince will be here soon. The reason to hide something is not so it isn't found but only found by those you want to find it.

She cleaned up the kitchen. Then took some wet cloths and went into the guest room and checked the window she had recently squirmed through.

"Glad I checked. Look at the dirt on the sill, sash, and outside." After cleaning away the evidence, she checked the floor, to make sure she didn't leave any dirt or boot prints there. The advantage of hardwood floors. Next, she walked to the parlor and removed two paintings. Then it was up the stairs to her work room closet, where she searched the paintings. There they are, now to switch them. Returning to her bedroom, she tore some paper from her sketch book and wrote on it, used a step stool to press an engraved rose on a bed post of her four-poster canopy bed. The carved rose slid to the side revealing a small hole. Agate placed the rolled-up paper in a hole, then pushed the rose back. Sub Rosa, my little prince. She replaced the step stool, made sure the place was neat and tidy, grabbed her duffel bag and then left by the same window.

Agate's House the Next Evening

The sun was setting as Zephrin pulled into Agate's driveway. Neatly trimmed hedges lined the walkway to the front door and a small, Spanish style windmill with a charging knight weathervane on top of it sat in the front yard. "It's identical to Paris, Baba, identical. The knight and windmill do your mother proud."

The company that moved and reassembled Agate's cottage, had done excellent work, even the orientation was the same, facing the rising sun. He closed his eyes, remembering a time long ago, outside of Paris.

***

A fancy carriage pulled up to the cottage, a Moor stepped down and opened the door for its young passenger.

"Your Highness."

"Thanks, Chalmers, I always like it that you speed up the carriage when I ask you to. How long has your family worked for my baba?" the young boy asked.

"You're most welcome, little Prince and to tell the truth, I enjoy doing it as well. We've served her since she purchased my family at auction. She set us free two years later. That would be oh, a little over thirty years ago now."

"Zephy, I'm in the kitchen, come help me with the strawberries," a female voice said from the front door. Zephrin took off running to the front door, throwing his arms around her.

***

The memory, and his purpose for being here, caused a tear to run down his cheek. He walked up to the front door. A name placard was hanging from the stone wall carved in the shape of an angel holding a rose; Ms. H. Agate d'Estange.

"That's different. It's been a long time since she used the H in her name."

The one and a half floor cottage with a middle section, located in the rear, as the second floor, stood out from all the others, like a castle in the middle of some peasant hovels. Made of stones held in place with mortar, it's French design so out of place, yet so familiar to Zephrin.

These American houses, for the most part, so bland, and unaesthetic. They aren't homes, just modern caves.

 He opened the door, shutting and locking it behind him. Parlor to the right, kitchen straight ahead with the bath and guest bedroom to the left off the kitchen. Door to the small patio and a pantry to the right off that door. He walked through the house, looking at the pictures, furniture, and other decorations, so neatly and tenderly placed. He ended at the kitchen.

So many good memories here. Mother was right, I've been very remiss by not keeping in regular contact with Agate and my parents.

Zephrin sat at the kitchen table, closed his eyes, and lightly rubbed his hand on the cherry tabletop.

Okay, Baba, speak to me. In his mind, the kitchen began to change like the frames of a movie reel.

***

He saw Agate by the sink, a metal hand pump faucet being used by a ten-year-old boy. The smell of fresh strawberries and bread filled his mind, causing him to salivate and lick his lips.

"Zephy, nice job helping me clean the strawberries. Would you like one?"

"Oh yes, Baba, can I roll it in sugar, like mommy does?"

"Oh no, Zephy, sugar hides the taste."

"Okay, I'll eat it without anything."

"Good choice. Now, it's time to do some painting. The weather is great, the sun is out, so let's paint back by the flower garden. I can see how much you remember about flowers."

"Of course, Baba," he held her hand as they walked outside.

I do enjoy eidetic memory. It's been particularly useful as a detective and Agate has it as well. All us vampires had something special. Are those specialties due to our long lives, in-breeding, or consuming our own blood? Even our scientists don't know about the last one. We can give and receive blood from other vampires via transfusions, in a pinch. It makes us lethargic for a day or so. A small percentage became extremely sick from it. Human blood, of course, we can receive with no complications. The Traditionalists have proven that when a human receives a transfusion of our blood, for the most part, it doesn't go well for the human. I've hunted two dozen feral vampires since Agate finished training me. I've never had to hunt a relative, one that I love very dearly.

**

He opened his eyes and the room returned to the present, like a backwards movie, frame by frame. The modern faucet, hardwood floors, modern doors and lights appeared.

"Okay, Baba, paintings and flowers," as he headed up stairs to her workshop.

CHAPTER 5

Lock 3 Park, a mecca for those desiring entertainment, music, and events year-round in Akron, Ohio. Though now mid-October, the weather was still comfortable, more like in late September. Jay Syne was the park's head grounds keeper and the last name on Agate's list. Agate entered the maintenance shed before closing, surprising a worker who'd had the unfortunate luck to be drinking whiskey. She doubted anyone heard his pathetic gurgling, as she grabbed a hand rake and drove its three semi pointed prongs into his neck. With nothing but time on her hands, she used it to put blood in her belly and sate the craving that was beginning to take more and more control of her. When finished, she splashed the whiskey on his body and dropped the flask on the ground. She sat the body on a chair and placed a pitchfork in his hands, holding it there for about two hours, until rigor mortis set in, the prongs pointing toward the door. Then she waited, perched on a shelf, above the door.

Jay Syne approached the shed the next morning.

"Carl, you left the god damn door open. Drunk on the job, again, I bet. You didn't even punch out. Well, you just earned yourself a weeklong suspension. We probably had everything stolen."

As Jay opened the door, entered the shed, and took a few steps in, he stepped on something tacky. He started to look down when Agate swung down hitting his back with her feet, forcing him, chest first, onto the pitchfork. Agate relished the sound of the tines sinking into Jay's chest, the blood flowing from the three holes and his pathetic attempts to pull himself off the pitchfork. She walked in front of him, the recognition of who she was shown in his eyes. She smiled and waved as he reached out to grab her.

"My mother's soul can finally rest. You're the last of Dulcinea murderers and torturers to have my revenge on. Oh, I do like your new name, Jason aka Jay Syne. So, tell me, does the pain help with your memory? What was that? The gurgling makes it hard to understand. I see the recognition in your eyes, though. You know what else I see…death; thank you so much for that. Watching you and the others die, I might have been wrong in thinking that there is such a thing as a noble death. If I may quote one of your ancestors, the last words you'll ever hear. Charles would take solace in them, hope you do as well.

"It is a far, far better thing that I do, than I have ever done; it is a far, far better rest that I go to, than I have ever known."

His efforts to speak produced frothy blood that gurgled from his mouth. She smiled as she taunted him, like a cat playing with a mouse, as he lost consciousness and the blackness of death overtook him. She put on his cap and a park cleaners' suit with a vest. Her blood-stained clothes from last night, she stuffed into her liter pouch. She put that over her shoulder, grabbed a pick stick and left the shed, promising to return what she borrowed, the next time she was in town. Next was planning for her trip to Warsaw.

Ashland, Ohio

The cleaning ladies returned and entered the house using the key Mr. Dunbar had given them. Once inside, they saw the house was in shambles, no not shambles, it had been trashed. They immediately called the police who arrived at Mike's house. It looked simple enough. The storm on Friday night had uprooted the tree, which had smashed the deck door open. Then some local kids must have climbed it and ransacked the place. There were empty beer bottles tossed around. Graffiti on the walls. The fridge and pantry had been raided. The place had been ransacked, a wall mounted TV and a computer had been taken. Probably any cash and jewelry they came across as well. To the arriving officers, that was the simple explanation. Yet, why was the alarm disabled if Mr. Dunbar wasn't home? They called it in to Captain Saunders, Ashland's Chief of Detectives.

Cecil, along with two investigators, arrived about ten minutes later.

"Okay, it appears to have been a robbery of opportunity. Dust for prints. Fred, you've the first floor, Laurie's up here with me."

Fred went downstairs with two officers. Cecil told one of the officers to contact the security firm and see what they could tell us about Mr. Dunbar's location. Then get his cell number and call him.

"Captain Saunders look at this," Laurie called.

Cecil came over to the phone and security panel, where the officer was.

"What did you find?"

"This partial print is different than all the others in the room."

Cecil looked at the rug, by the wall. Yes, it did look different, only a partial print, the front part of a boot with a sneaker print on top of it.

"Okay, get forensics here and do the routine. Check to see if there are any more boot prints in the house that match this one. Looks like another person was here before the kids. If that's true, there should be more boot prints. Call in some uniformed officers to check with the neighbors. Make sure they dust for prints on the phone, security panel, and furniture. Anyone find out where Mr. Dunbar is and works?"

"Sir," one of the responding officers said. "He works at the University in the Records and Transcripts as assistant director."

"Contact them as well. Now, it's time for me to interview the cleaning crew."

***

Laurent Fortesque arrived at The Ashland Center for English Studies and met with the Muslim students at an arranged luncheon. The President of Ashland University, Jean Kirkland, was there as well. The students had done an excellent job, preparing for his arrival. The food was prepared by halal standards and, before dinner, there was the Asr time of prayer. When the meal was over, it was time for him to speak. Laurent got up from his seat on the dais and moved to the podium.

"I thank you, President Kirkland and the fine students of Ashland University, for your welcome. I know that all here are not of the Islamic faith, which shows that in America, you are free to practice your Islamic, Christian, Jewish, Hindu or any faith, of ones choosing. Yet, as important as that freedom is, how free are Muslims in America today? That is the reason for me being here. To find out from you, what it's like being Muslim in middle America. What makes you feel free? What problems do you encounter? How are you treated by your fellow students and residents? Do you have non-Muslim friends? What do your parents say? What made you friends with them and them with you? What do you talk about and do with them? What teachers do you or don't you like, and why? What are your favorite TV shows and least favorite?"

Laurent spent about forty-five minutes, listening to their answers, and replying to some questions. They had language issues and, as expected, a misunderstanding about Islam. They were treated well by their fellow students. Most had non-Muslim friends, some had joined campus fraternities or sororities. There were twelve or so who had non-Muslim boyfriends or girlfriends. One young man said sharing classes and experiences had helped him make friends. Americans, though they didn't seem to know they did this, separated faith, and religion. One young girl had mentioned that Americans like you the more you don't look and act different. They don't understand differences, though they don't mind you being a little different.

Laurent felt a small pang of regret, small but he did feel it.

   This is going to make an interesting article, I'm a bit humbled by their honesty and friendship, all in the name of showing America what Islam and being Muslin is like. Pity that my real purpose here makes that secondary. Fortunately, a story is expected, and not only will it help with my cover, I'm going to make it a really great story, so I may as well find out what I talked about in my speech.

After they were done. "Well my friends, I'm surprised by your willingness to take part and honesty of your answers. I'll admit that while I was driving here, I attempted to anticipate your answers and questions. I didn't do that good of a job. However, I do have an article to write. If several of you would be willing to provide me a tour of your campus in the morning, I'd greatly appreciate that." Laurent made sure that those who asked the best questions or gave the best answers, were selected for the tour.

The next morning, Laurent and his tour guides spent several hours traversing the campus. They showed him the science and language arts buildings, their dorms and talked about their classes, the food, and local places they liked to hang out. They added in all that they did and didn't like at

Ashland. They finished at the Student Union, where Laurent got coffee, drinks, and sandwiches for all. Laurent took a sip of his coffee and did a job worthy of an academy award, so as not to choke on it. He thanked them for their time and answers, as he finished up any questions they had.

"Are any here art majors? I ask because art is expressionist, it shows and evokes emotion, from the creator and those who view it. Emotion knows no faith, nationality, ethnicity or language."

"Mr. Fortesque, my name is Afnan and I'm an art major," replied a raven-haired girl with hazel eyes. She'd been the girl who talked about blending in last night. In support of that premise, she wasn't wearing a hijab and had dressed in a most American style that showed her figure, jeans and a long sleeve shirt. He smiled at her.

"Do you have anything on display?"

"Why yes, some black and white photographs and a few pencil sketches, at the Arts and Humanities building."

"I'd love to see them. Would you please show them to me?"

"Sure." Afnan led the two of them there, as Laurent brushed his hand over hers.

CHAPTER 6

Funk Bottoms

Matt had been fishing since before the sun had come up. The day was more in line with late October. It was about 40 degrees Fahrenheit, instead of the upper 50's of the previous weeks, when Matt rowed to a dry mound to relieve himself of the beer that had started the day with him. He went to a clump of bushes and began his steam of urine, yet it didn't sound right. He noticed the flies and a stench, like that of roadkill. He finished his business and moved some of the branches and saw the mutilated body. He let loose a scream as he turned and retched, his stomach emptying its contents on the ground nearby. A few minutes later, as his stomach calmed down, he called 911.

"911, what is the nature of your emergency?"

"I'm at Funk Bottoms and I just found a dead body."

The call was routed to the Ashland County Sheriff's office and taken by Deputy Richard Lambert.

"Deputy Lambert here, please give me your name, location and emergency."

"Yeah hello, I'm Matt Grayson. Oh, I'm at Funk Bottoms, on an island and I found a dead body."

"Matt, please slow down and repeat what you just told me."

Rich grabbed a pad and pen and began writing.

"Dead body, male, foot caught in an animal trap, stinks and covered with flies, you pissed on it. Okay, stay there, I'll send some deputies to meet you. Don't touch anything, Matt. Thanks for calling."

The Ashland County Medical Examiner's van pulled up next to the sheriff's cruiser. Two county sheriffs and a kid were standing near a picnic table, the kid was sitting on it. Zarkof Tashkent and two others emerged from the van and greeted Tom and Sherrie.

"Dr. Zarkof, I've got Matt Grayson's statement. He'd been fishing from about 4:30 this morning when he went to relieve himself and found the body. His boat checks with that as there were several perch in a sieve container. He works at the Archway plant and is on vacation this week."

"Thanks, Tom. Which island is the body on?"

"The one on the right, about 2 O'clock from us. You might see that marker pole we put up. The body is in those bushes. There's also a tent and camp on another island, at 12 O'clock."

"I'll go to the body with you and one technician. Sherrie, you take the other tech and go to the camp. Did Matt disturb the scene?"

"He says that once he called us, the only thing he did was get off the island. He did say that he had pissed on the body before he saw it."

"Well, not as bad as it might have been."

Dr. Zarkof, Tom and Dave, had no trouble locating the body. He walked around it several times, looking at it while writing notes. He put his note pad away and opened his examination kit.

"Dave, make sure you get pictures, especially a close up of that neck bite, that's the worst of them."

"Well Doctor, what do you think happened?"

"I'm not sure yet, Tom. Very confusing. The victim is a white male between 30 and 35 years of age. He's been dead about two maybe three days and there is ample evidence of being eaten by animals. His right foot is in a fox trap, though that wasn't the cause of death. Looks like coyotes, maybe a small bear along with smaller creatures fed off the body. He was in a fight; his left arm is broken. That's an interesting bite and tear on his neck, maybe a badger but I don't think so. I'll know more once he's back at the lab, but I think that was what killed him. None of the other bite marks are fatal. That bite was on the jugular, yet not much blood on the body. I don't think he was killed here. Is there any I.D. on him?"

"No, but if he wasn't killed here, how did he get his foot caught in a bear trap?"

"Fox trap, that's a fox trap, Tom, which also puzzles me. He would have screamed his head off from the pain but should have been able to call for help or just reset the trap and pull his leg out."

Tom's radio came on, "Tom, Sherrie here. We're at the camp site. ID in the tent belongs to a Mike Dunbar, male

Caucasian, thirty-two years old. Lives at 12 West Woodhill Drive, Ashland. Looks like he was camping and trapping, found a couple of traps and other gear.

The camp's torn up. I've called in help to bag and picture it."

Ashland, Ohio

While searching Agate's work room, Zephrin didn't see anything unusual or disturbed.

"All is as I'd expect it to be. I see she's arranged for someone to watch her house while she's gone. The plants have been watered and the place is clean. Need to find that someone."

He walked around looking at the painting on the easel, barely started, only an unplowed field so far, as he noticed the smell of honeysuckle. "Baba did like to use scents in her colors, that would be the wildflowers. He opened a small closet that had two well used painting smocks, a beret, and several palettes. On the floor was a heavy cloth covering some stuff. He removed the cloth and saw several framed canvas paintings. One was of a woman, mid to late twenties, sitting on a bench in front of a building, holding some flowers. Her skin was medium brown with straight, shoulder-length hair, brown with a red tint. Zephrin nodded, the subject of the painting was attractive. The vase held Queen Ann's Lace, White and Purple Heather and a White Rose, all flowers Baba liked. Zephrin noticed some dust on the top of its framework and on one other but none on the other paintings. Those two paintings had been hanging up recently. The other was of Zephrin, playing in the orchard, the one with six of him. It was one of Agate's favorites. She had written my name on the trees, one letter on each tree, hidden in the bark. She told me that if I could find all the letters in five minutes, she'd make my favorite pie, lemon custard. I didn't have pie for desert that night. Who and why had they taken them down and put them here? Queen Ann's Lace, the wild carrot, she even put the purple flower in the middle. Don't remember what it means. White and Purple Heather mean beauty and dreaming, I think. The White Rose could be any of honor, beauty, innocence, and purity.

Zephrin went back downstairs and, in the guest bedroom, saw a painting of his mother, with roses he'd cut from her garden for his mom's one hundred and fiftieth birthday, and another of his great grand uncle's castle in Romania. He also noticed that the frame had no dust on it. "Now why switch these two paintings?"

He then went back to the art studio. "The captain did say I could take pictures, though I'm sure he meant with a camera and not with my hands, but even more importantly they were recently changed and only Baba or the person who's taking care of her house could have done that," he said to no one in particular as he placed the two paintings from upstairs into his car.

***

While touring the Art center, Afnan had returned Laurent's flirtations. He was impressed with the works he saw because frankly, he had expected trash. The artwork wasn't bad, by European standards, and Afnan's black and white pictures were okay, but her pencil sketches were exceptionally good, professional level. These students and professors thought it was much better and that's an example of Americans' unintentional arrogance in their own accomplishments. What caught his eye was some faience blanche pottery. A table setting with a creamer. He read the plate which identified the maker, Ms. Agate d'Estange, professor of Art and Art History. My oh my! Betrayed by a table setting and a creamer. How funny that the things we love are so dangerous. So, now you call yourself Agate. No more Henriette. You're who Mike found and was investigating. You found out and disappeared. Most likely I'll never be able to meet Mr. Dunbar. C'est la vie.

"Mr. Fortesque are you okay," Afnan asked.

"I was surprised to see such a fine example of faience blanche pottery."

"Oh, yes, professor d'Estange makes some very pretty pieces. Did you know that she studied in Paris before coming here?"

"No, I didn't, did she study at Sorbonne?"

"I don't know the name of the school, Mr. Fortesque."

"Could I meet with her?"

"No, she had to go tend to a dead sister's funeral."

"Where did she have to go?"

"Bulgaria."

That night, in his hotel room, Laurent cuddled Afnan in his arms. "So, Ms. Kamani, how has the drought hurt your father's cassava farm?"

"The yield might be down from ten to twenty percent. That would keep me from returning to Ashland for my senior year. He's talking about finding a husband for me in either case."

"That would be a waste, what if I was able to see your final year was paid for?"

Afnan sat up in surprise. "Really?"

With a smile and nod, Laurent said, "Indeed."

"I'll let my parents know."

"Tell your parents that you received a scholarship for your artwork. Continue to get a 3.5 GPA. Take as many journalism classes as you can and work on your drawings. After you graduate you could become a reporter or sketch artist for Al-Jazeera America."

"Would I have to move to New York City and what do I do if my dad finds a husband for me?"

"Not sure, but we'll figure that out after you graduate. Find some nice American boy and have him fall in love with you, then be a faithful wife."

"Okay," she moved her hand down to squeeze him, enjoying his growing size. She kissed him on his lips and continued down his neck, lightly blowing and humming.

"Very nice," Laurent said.

Afnan took Laurent into her mouth. Laurent made small thrusts with his hips. She gave a seductive glance at Laurent, enjoying the look on his face. Laurent's gasps were enthralling when she resumed pleasuring him with tongue and fingers.

"Yes, my dear Afnan, you are a fantastic lover," Laurent said.

Afnan shifted to a sixty-nine position. They teased and enjoyed each other's ministrations and, after several more minutes, both enjoyed the blissful joy of an orgasm. Laurent held Afnan, caressing her back and playing with her hair, until she fell asleep. A half hour later, Laurent got out of bed without waking her and went to his computer to finish his article. Speaking in Esperanto, the vampire language, just in case.

"Good, a genuinely nice article and I must admit that I learned something. Younger Muslims here are treated well by their non-Muslim peers. True, they get some side-eyes and epitaphs tossed their way, but they feel honest acceptance from most of their fellow students. They feed off it, drifting from the traditional teachings of Islam. They haven't slipped in their Islamic beliefs. These student's, unknowingly, have become Americanized. They have developed a schism between what one's faith is and what one's religion or the codified practice of celebrating the faith is. I could tell that their belief was unchanged. It's such a pity that the Iman's and Ayatollah's don't consider this." There was a stirring from the bed, and he looked over at Afnan. Well, for the most part Afnan and I share a common thread, we both don't care as much about our religion as we show.

He then took out one of his cell phones and punched in a number. Remembering to speak in Esperanto, he heard.

"Thank you for calling San Guine Pharmaceuticals. Our directory has recently changed. If you know your party's extension, you may enter it at any time."

Laurent entered a seven-digit number.

"Name please."

"Laurent Fortesque."

"Voice print and pattern confirmed. Please hold the camera so that your retinal print can be confirmed."

He did so.

"Retinal print confirmed. Greetings Under Director Laurent Fortesque, Director Daniels will be with you shortly."

"Thanks."

About fifteen seconds later, Dr. Daniels answered.

"Laurent, long time. How's everything going?"

"As for my job, rather well. First, I want you to do something for me, Javier."

"Sure Laurent, what do you need?'

"There is a young student at Ashland University, in Ohio, Afnan Kamani. See that her next year's college expenses are paid for."

"Laurent, using your skill to rock the cradle, at your age?"

"I used no skill, until we were in bed and her skill wasn't bad either. That, and now Al-Jazeera has a new reporter. Now for business. Unfortunately, there's been an unexpected life changing event. I would strongly recommend that you prepare a response team for the death of Mike Dunbar, of Ashland, Ohio."

"Why? Did he make you upset?"

"Not me, Javier, somebody else. One Henriette Tangre, now going by Agate d'Estange. The one I've been searching for. He discovered a vampire and some of her past, unfortunately, she discovered him. I'd bet that he's dead. Agate is missing. She told a professor who's taking over her classes that she had to go to Bulgaria for a sister's funeral. She has no sister, but a daughter who lives in Sofia, and a grandson you might have heard of, Zephrin Ivano."

"Crap!"

"Even worse, she might even know about Dunbar's team and the team could be in danger."

"Okay, I'll send a flash evacuation bulletin for them. Next, what to do about Ivano's parents? We have to assume they know about us."

"We do nothing about them. They are in Bulgaria, leave them there and I mean that."

"Okay, Laurent. How long will you be there, because I can have a response team there in three days, to capture or terminate Zephrin?"

"I'll be here but no crew, only one person. Javier, you know how we play this game. Just because a valuable piece is vulnerable, doesn't mean it's not protected. What would we lose to capture it? What problems would result? Right now, we'd be on the wrong side of the joint council's decision. You remember, the one that shut down your human R&D facility. Besides, I don't want a war."

"Okay, Laurent, you're right, no time to start a war."

"We'll just be happy with the 'little accidents' that happen to each side. Okay, one person. Let me think here...yeah, I'll send Jania Mikos, I'll send her encrypted file to you. I've a few contacts at the State Department. I'll know if Zephrin has entered the country and any other information about his location. We can't let them find out our location, Laurent, yet why don't we want a direct confrontation?"

"Javier, our last one wasn't pretty. The lack of technology made it much easier to hide our motives, connections, and manipulations. A new war wouldn't be as easy, and we're not prepared. That, and I want Zephrin alone, not a team with me. It'll be me and him, with his skull ending up in my collection."

"Interesting logic and a valid point. Just remember that Modernists also aren't prepared for war. Protect yourselves and our secret. If some die along the way, so be it."

After the connection ended, Javier said, "It's better to act quickly and err, than to hesitate until the time of action is past. That was one of grand dads' better ones."

CHAPTER 7

Ashland University

Cecil knocked on Brielle Chalmers's office door. "Come in, my door is always open for students."

As Cecil entered her office, it was just as inviting as before. Several small rugs on the floor, some potted flowers and two leather chairs.

"Wish I was a student, but I draw stick people so I'm very good at hang man."

"Why, you're Detective Saunders. Don't knock that, have you ever tried to really draw? If not, try it. You talked to me about Agate's disappearance a couple of weeks ago, didn't you? I see you're still wearing that Browns pin."

"Good morning, Miss Chalmers, yes, I'm Detective Saunders, but you can call me Cecil. I called yesterday about meeting with you and I've always had a Browns pin."

"Oh my, I had forgotten, so sorry. Yes, please have a seat, Cecil, how can I help you today?"

"I have some questions about Agate's missing person report to go over with you," he said as he sat in one of the leather chairs.

"What do you mean missing? She's in Bulgaria attending the funeral of her sister and tending to the estate."

"She is? I thought she was missing. Why didn't you contact the police, didn't you know we had a missing person's report on her?"

"Didn't she call your office? She called me what, three maybe four days ago saying that she apologized for her abrupt leaving, but that her sister had died in a car accident and that she had to go to Sofia for the funeral and take care of her sister's estate. She said that she'd call the police to let them know."

"No, Professor d'Estange hasn't contacted our department. So, Agate d'Estange is no longer a missing person?"

"Why, I'd think not, since I know where she is, Cecil."

"Did Agate give you a contact number or time that she would be back? Did she call you at home or your cell phone? We've called her cell phone, but it's turned off."

"Why no, she didn't give me a contact number. She said she'd return when she'd finished taking care of business, she hoped in about two weeks. She called my home number."

"I'll see if I can get the records about where and when she called. A few more questions. Since she told you that she'd be back but, at least so far, hasn't contacted anyone else. Do you know if she had any enemies? Who did you tell about his? Were there any students or fellow professors who didn't like her? Oh, did she mention if she contacted the University?"

"No, Cecil, I'm not aware of any who didn't like her. I did tell her classes as she asked me to cover for her. There are always students who don't like a grade they receive. She was well liked by almost all her students and respected by her peers. I said earlier that she did tell me she'd contact the University but not when or if she had."

"Thanks, Ms. Chalmers, sorry for having to bother you."

Chuck Thompkins was listening to Nova Home Security's copy of the call they received from Mike Dunbar's home. Nova had included a transcript of the recording as well. Mike Dunbar's home alarm system had flashed for a broken door at 6:49pm. At 6:53pm, the security code was entered, an automatic call was made. At 6:55pm, Mike Dunbar had answered, his voice being verified by voice print.

"Yes, a tree in my back yard was toppled by the high winds and broke a glass sliding door, that's all. I'll call my insurance company in the morning."

"Okay Mr. Dunbar, voice analysis is confirmed, have a good evening."

"Thank you, sir, and I hope you have a good evening as well."

"Well," Chuck said speaking out loud and jotting down notes about the case. "I'll get tech to analyze the recording and verify the voice, it sounds legit. The insurance company says they haven't received any communication from Mr. Dunbar. His death is a homicide, based on evidence at the scene where the body was found. We also have a non-missing person. See what relationship the professor had with Mr. Dunbar. Contact the daughter to see if she's heard from her mother."

Chuck put that transcript and copy aside and grabbed the notes about Mr. Dunbar. Mike Dunbar's Ford Transit, was found in the parking lot, still locked. It was being checked along with the GPS to see when and how far it had been driven. Were any calls made from its Blue tooth system? Forensics was checking for prints, just in case. He was impatiently waiting for Zarkof to finish the autopsy, the teeth marks on his pencil, testimony to his impatience. He'd sent the official request for Mr. Dunbar's medical records, along with next of kin contact numbers. There was a knocking on the frame of his door, Cecil's head was poking around the side.

"I've got some information from Mike Dunbar's house; you'll find it interesting but I'm not sure you'll like it."

"Okay, have a seat and give."

"Forensics provided its findings. They found prints of a right index and middle finger on the phone. They were run through the criminal data base, with no matches. Next, a partial boot print was found by the phone/security panel and evidence of even smaller parts of boot prints, only in the master bedroom. None of the kids arrested for stealing were wearing anything that matched. We ran it through a data base, it came up as a Harley Davidson Leather Riding boot, possibly a lady's boot."

"So, you're suggesting..."

"Someone else was in that room, before the kids, and it might have been a lady."

"Okay, then how would you explain Mike's voice on the Nova Security tape? Were there any matching prints on the security panel?"

"They couldn't pull any clear prints from the panel. I can't figure Mike's voice on the Nova recording out yet, but maybe it was a ventriloquist."

"Run those fingerprints through the State Department. We've an international student base, so maybe one of them."

***

For the third time, Zephrin was trying to follow the verbal directions of students, to the Art and Humanities Center. So far, he'd found three dumpsters, two dorm complexes, the Student Union, and the gymnasium, on his hiking expeditions. He'd even refused an offer of help from a student to take him there. I own an international detective agency, but I can't find my way around a small, middle of no place, college campus. That's embarrassing.

However, this time his orienteering met with success. He'd already been given a key to Agate's office by campus security, on the third floor. He went in to look around and saw what he expected, a very neat office, some chrysanthemums in a Japanese vase on her desk. Life and rebirth, genuinely nice, Baba. The water in the vase was fresh. He sat at the desk and began looking through her Rolodex. Why so old fashion, Baba? Names and numbers with notes in both French and Bulgarian, saying student or teacher. Some good and bad for food places and building help. He was going through her file cabinet when he was interrupted, by a throat clearing noise.

"Just who the hell are you and what the hell are you doing in this office?"

Zephrin looked up and saw a lady staring back at him, arms folded in front of her, with a look his mother would've given him for doing something wrong and bad, at the same time. She also seemed familiar. Where have I seen her before? Medium brown skin, straight brown hair, with red tint, and hazel eyes.

"My name is Zephrin Ivano. I'm a detective hired by Ms. d'Estange's daughter to investigate her disappearance. Campus security provided me with a key. Who are you?"

"I'm Brielle Chalmers, and she'd asked me to cover for her. Now, since she told me why she was gone and where she was going, I know you're a liar. Now get the hell out of here before I call the police," she said as she pulled her cell phone out.

"Well Ms. Chalmers, you of course can call the police, I met Chief Thompkins the other day, or you can tell me why you think I'm a liar."

"As I told Cecil yesterday, Agate had called me a few days ago. She had to go back to Bulgaria, for her sister's funeral and to handle the estate. I'd think her daughter would know if her aunt had died, don't you?"

"Most interesting and correct, if Ms. d'Estange had a sister, but she doesn't. So, are you sure it was Ms. d'Estange?" He stood up and walked around the desk.

"Well I'm sure it was her, detective." as Brielle moved to keep the desk between them. It was when the vase of flowers was in front of her...That's it!

"Ms. Chalmers, please call me Zephrin. Have you ever posed for a portrait for Agate, I mean Ms. d'Estange?"

"Yes, I have. It was this August, before school started."

"Can you describe the portrait?"

"That's easy, it was in front of the Student Union. I was holding a cup of coffee, but she put some flowers in my hand instead. She said they accented my eyes and hair, and you may call me Brielle."

"The painting doesn't do you justice. I saw it when I looked over Agate's house last night. Brielle, if you have some time, could you tell me what Agate was like recently? You've had the most recent contact with her. My client, her daughter, has informed me that she has no sisters and feels she is missing. Please, tell me what you can. I'll even buy coffee at the Student Union, to which I know how to get to."

"Okay, let's walk."

They left the building and headed to the Student Union. Zephrin bought coffee and bagels.

"It was close to three weeks now, when she first didn't show for her class, that was a Tuesday. The police investigated a missing person's report that Friday. They interviewed all the staff. Nobody knew anything. I know they checked her house. I was there. She'd given me a key for when she was out of town, to take care of her cottage, plants, and the flower garden. They took pictures and listened to the answering machine. There were several messages from students and a couple from fellow teachers. There were a few messages in French and another foreign language, but that's all I know. Then, last Sunday night, she called me saying that she had gone back home, to Sofia, Bulgaria to attend her sister's funeral and to take care of her estate. She asked me to take over her classes while she was out."

Zephrin took a sip of coffee. What is it about America and what they think coffee is?

"Did you call in the missing person report?" That was the night mom called me, about Agate.

"No, that wasn't me and I don't know who did. She's well-liked by students and her colleagues."

"Had she ever asked you to cover her classes before?"

"No. She's never missed a class since I've been here, about eleven years now, first as her student then as a professor. She'd asked me several times to watch her plants for the weekend."

"Did Agate ever talk about her family and did you change two of the paintings in the house?"

"She talked about a daughter in Sofia and her grandson. I don't remember where he lives. She had several paintings with him as a little boy in them and no, why would I move her paintings around?"

"So, she never mentioned a sister when you talked?"

"Why no, she didn't, Zephrin. Now I've a few questions for you."

"Only fair, ask me."

"Where does her daughter live, and you live?"

"Sofia, Bulgaria. I live in Venice, Italy and am a detective employed by the International Security Investigation Agency, which was hired by her daughter to investigate."

"Why an Italian citizen? Don't they have good detectives in America?"

"Do I have an Italian accent?"

"No, you don't, but most American's don't use their hands when talking like you do."

"That's very observant of you, Ms. Chalmers."

***

Afnan and Laurent, were heading for the Arts and Humanities building, so he could see more of her art. Laurent saw a remarkably familiar face, Zephrin Ivano. He was a little worried but also convinced about Agate's identity.

"Afnan, you wouldn't know who those two professors are, heading for the Student Union, would you? One looks familiar to me," as he gestured toward Zephrin and Brielle.

"Well the lady is Brielle Chalmers. You probably saw her picture in the A & H building. She's the professor who took over Professor Agate's classes. I don't know who she's with."

"Why thanks very much." I know who he is. I so love the element of surprise, mon amie and I can't say or do anything right now, but soon.

CHAPTER 8

Ashland, Ohio

Zarkof, was in the examining room, doing the autopsy. His headset was on and hooked to his I-Pad, to record the autopsy along with an old-fashioned tape recorder.

"Hey, Hans, got anything for me?" Chuck Thompkins asked as he entered the examination room.

"Be quiet, you fool! Do you want Emperor Ming to hear you and destroy all our plans? How else are we going to save the Earth?" The man doing the examination said, looking toward Chuck, his eyes narrowing.

Chuck blinked, then saw a smile appear on Zarkof's face.

"Okay, you got me, but how? You hate sci-fi."

"True, but I figured it would be best to know the reference. The movie didn't have much more than the end as a redeeming quality. Oh, and you don't have the reference correct, unless you're attempting to insult me. Watch the movie again, so that you get it right. It was good seeing your reaction to my response."

"I'm sorry, I was only kidding with that reference."

"In answer to your question, I do. Mr. Dunbar was in a fight before he died, broken nose, right thigh bone and right radius, all very recent. Yet, his left leg, just above the ankle, was in a fox trap, that trap was on another small island. Chuck, he didn't step in the trap and then die. If he was alive, these injuries would've made it impossible for him to get to the island we found him on. He was dead when his foot was put in the trap. Besides the broken bones, his body had signs of bruising, consistent with a fight. Mr. Dunbar was murdered, and it was personal, very personal. The funny thing is, despite his severe injuries, those wouldn't have killed him. Something took a bite out of the front of his throat and that killed him. He bled to death."

"Okay, so he's beat to a pulp and knocked out. While on the ground an animal comes along and bites him in the neck?"

"Doubt it. That would mean the person he had a fight with came back after an animal killed him and moved the body. Why leave? The size of the bite is small. I'm unable to make a cast but I'd bet that it was a human bite, not an animal. To support that, there were no claw marks on the body. In my medical opinion, another person, after having a fight with Mike Dunbar, bit him in the neck, killing him, and then transported the body to the island where he was found. The full blood work should be ready in a couple of days."

"You're kidding me. You're suggesting that a person killed Mr. Dunbar by biting him the neck? Now, tell me the real reason."

"Chuck, I just did. Being honest, that would be a murder weapon. If that body had been outside another 48 hrs. I wouldn't have known he'd been bitten. I'd known he was murdered but not how."

**

Humans are so much like us, in some respects. We can smell blood, the fresher, the easier. They can smell money, the larger, the easier.

Laurent thought as he met the three pawns he intended to sacrifice in the game. He was at the Go Oasis truck stop, off US 250 and Interstate 71, outside of Ashland.

"Gentlemen, do you understand what I'm asking of you?" Laurent asked.

"Of course," Dave said. "I'll tail the couple and report what they do, while you, Terry and Sam get into the house and check it out. You got our money?"

Laurent handed them each an envelope. "Feel free to check. Also, Terry and Sam, wear gloves, and no stealing or ransacking of the house. I'm investigating and don't want any evidence left behind."

"Gotcha," Sam and Terry said.

"Who am I tailing?"

Laurent handed Dave pictures of Brielle and Ivano, with their names on them.

"The man is an expert in martial arts. Don't get stupid and think a knife or gun will scare him into giving up their money, which as a tourist, he does carry. However, once

I've completed my search of the house, if you wish to amuse yourselves, go ahead."

***

After Brielle and Zephrin had finished asking and answering questions about Agate and each other, she suggested they go to Eva's Treats for a burger and ice cream, on her.

"Give you a chance to relax and see a bit more of Ashland. Maybe the coffee will be better, you never finished what you had at the Student Union."

"Was I that obvious?"

"Not really, but I'm good at reading people and knowing you're Italian and how that culture has a coffee sub-culture, I could tell. Thanks for hiding it."

They spent almost forty-five minutes eating and talking. Zephrin did try another coffee. It was better, so he did finish the cup, while enjoying the pleasurable time with Brielle. A relaxing break in a confusing case.

I can see why Baba likes her. Her personality matches her good looks. Excellent conversationalist, polite, smart, well mannered, and observant. The kind of girl everyone's mother would like… especially mine. Was Baba thinking of being a matchmaker? Maybe, but that's not a reason for her to move here to teach.

"Well Zephrin, I need to check on Agate's flowers, then get home, I do have some young minds to instruct after the sun comes up."

"Of course, Brielle. Would it be okay if I escorted you to Agate's house and then saw you to yours?"

"Why, that's so charming, old fashion and well, nice, Zephrin, it would also be very welcome."

They reached Agate's house, in about thirty minutes. Brielle opened the door.

Zephrin's eyes widened. He smelled something faint that wasn't there when he was here earlier.

Guerlain, a European cologne, that's what I smell. Someone's been here, recently.

"Brielle, does everything look okay?"

"Yes, why do you ask?"

"Oh, I thought I smelled something, that's all."

"I did as well when we entered the kitchen. Thought it was your cologne, but yours is different."

She smelled it also, and she's familiar with this house and its smells. This place has been searched. Someone was looking for something, very carefully.

Brielle, watered the plants, checked the refrigerator for any food that she might have missed, that could spoil. Then she walked through each room, checking.

"Is this how you normally check when house sitting," Zephrin asked, slightly joking.

"Yes, why, wouldn't you? She called me her little curator, not a house sitter."

"No, I didn't mean it that way. I'm impressed that you did that and yes, I agree with Agate calling you a curator."

CHAPTER 9

Akron, Ohio

The Akron police had cordoned off the area around a storage shed, at Lock 3 Park. The coroner's office was sweeping a fifty-foot radius from the shed, taking pictures and bagging anything that looked out of place. Yet, the interesting work was inside the shed, with the two dead bodies.

"Robin, tell me what we have here," said Lt. Bill Richards.

"I'll do my best. We have two murder victims. The first victim is the one sitting, holding the pitchfork, Carl Jeffers, forty-five. He was killed sometime between 6:00 and 8:00pm last night. Someone planted that three-prong garden rake into his neck. The second dead body, the one on the pitchfork, is his boss, Jay Syne, thirty-six. Jay was killed when he was forcibly impaled on the pitchfork, between 5:00 and 6:00am this morning. They were discovered by Chen Lou at about 8:10am, when she entered the shed."

"Impaled? How does a dead man impale anyone?"

"Haven't figured that part out yet, but I'd bet the killer was still in the shed. Probably on that ledge above the door or behind it when it was opened. Mr. Syne entered the shed, they slam themselves on his back which drives him into the pitchfork."

"You think they were killed by the same person?"

"I'd bet on it. I can't give you a motive. Whiskey was found spilled on the floor and Carl has a history of drinking including two trips to AA. Jay had threatened Carl with termination, if ever drunk or drinking at work."

"Does Carl have any relatives?"

"That's being looked into. Records indicate that Carl had been married, divorced three years ago. Jay was single. Officers are en-route to each of their residences."

"Okay, what about the murderer?"

"Nothing much on that yet. As I said, I think that Jay was struck from above and or behind. Carl was struck from the front. Due to the difference in body temperature, my bet is the killer entered the shed near closing. They surprised Carl, who they killed with the three-prong hand rake. This isn't that big of a shed. Most likely any struggle would've made a mess of it. Hence, Carl being surprised. That's why I think that Jay was the target. We're checking his background as being more important. There were multiple footprints in the blood, all exiting the shed. Those are being checked but they look like a boot print. Chen says that a park services uniform, pick stick and collection bag are missing. The security cameras are being checked to see what they will show us. These were brutal murders, yet some confusing aspects. See the blood spray on the walls?"

Bill turned and looked, saw that the spray covered a wide area and then nodded.

"Those are from Carl. However, I'd expect to see much more on the floor, and I don't. It covers most of Carl's shirt and his pants but there should be more. Where did it go? The average human body has about five quarts of blood. Oh well, another mystery to fathom about later. My guess is that the murderer propped Carl's body on that chair and arranged it to hold the pitchfork. Why? I'd say that they knew Jay would be coming. Having a pitchfork buried in your chest is a very painful and slow way to die and would explain why he didn't scream his head off, a pitchfork in your lungs, might have prevented that. Their wallets and watches are still on them, so we can rule out robbery and, so far, no drugs have been found. I'll do my autopsy and let you know in a couple of days, Bill."

Seneca Caves, Bellevue, Ohio

Charlie had the pleasure of taking the last group of the year, though the caves. There were eleven or twelve people, including two kids, who looked to be between ten and twelve.

"Your attention please, as we descend into the caves. There are walkways that you should stay on and some areas where you can explore and climb. Many areas are tight fits, so if you are claustrophobic, please let me know. The caves were discovered in 1872 by Peter Rutan and Henry Homer, who were out rabbit hunting. The Foyer where we will start, is twenty feet underground. Yes, for those who might have a concern, we might find some bats. No need to worry, Dracula was denied entry into the country by

Homeland Security." This produced a laugh, which even Agate agreed with.

The group continued to the Fossil Room.

"Hey, Mommy, look at the bones in the stone. How did they get there?" A young girl asked.

"Well, little girl, this is the Fossil Room and many nice fossils have been found and are for sale in the gift shop. If anyone happens to pick up a fossil from a rock they see, go ahead. We are now thirty feet underground. Please remember to stay on the walkway, so you don't get injured. Our next stop is Chert Alley and that's about fifty feet underground."

The tight squeezes were more common than Agate remembered from her earlier trips. The old graffiti in the Hall of Inscriptions was nice, yet the stalactites, were a bit of a letdown. There were a lot of them, but they were small, maybe a couple of inches long. There were some raw gemstones, semi-precious at best, in some of the rocks. The subdued lighting and natural beauty, an excellent enhancement to the area. Agate was interested in the area called Devil's Leap for later. Cathedral Hall was the biggest place, maybe nine feet high. There were many small crawl areas where no one was supposed to go. The group continued and, as it was autumn, they were able to get to Ole Mist'ry River. A fancy name for the water table, it was crystal clear and cold. Charlie informed them that they were about 110 feet underground.

On their way back. Agate slipped away from the group and headed back to Devil's Leap. She jumped to the wall, climbing down to the Wild Cave area. Since there were no tours here, this was a place where she could hide until her rescuers came. She pressed a button on a pager. So much had gone wrong. She could feel the Fangs of Death, creeping through her body and mind. She knew that 'Agate' was still there fighting it. How did she know this? The pain, oh the pain.

Ashland, Ohio

Brielle finished checking on the plants in about fifteen minutes and they started walking to her house. They took a path to a small bridge over Town Run, then headed to Brielle's house, on Ashland Ave. They were talking about Brielle being one of Agate's students, earning a Tutorial Assistant position, under Agate. After graduation, she became an adjunct professor, then full professor. Zephrin had offered his arm, as he walked on the street side of the sidewalk. Brielle had smiled, saying how quaint, old fashioned, gallant, and chivalrous that was. "You're a bit like Don Quixote, out of place in the world, yet a breath of fresh air. Did you know that Agate liked Cervantes and Casanova?"

Of course, I do. "No, her daughter didn't tell me that."

"Oh, yes, she has some of Cervantes's books, in Spanish but she really liked Casanova. She had all his stuff and in French and Italian."

About half-way there, three men appeared from behind some bushes. They were dressed in leather jackets, one had a pistol, the others had switchblades. Brielle's hand went to her mouth, her other grabbed Zephrin's arm. Zephrin was livid, being caught flatfooted, like a rookie. He was limited in his ability to react, with Brielle right next to him. His face flushed red and eyes narrowed, as he looked at all three of them. The one who was the calmest, was the one with the gun. The gunman is the leader, he needs to go first. The gunman spoke.

"There, there now, good friends. You see, granted, it's a bit early, but we're collecting for the Red Kettle drive this year. Would you be so kind as to give us your wallets, purses, rings, and such? I promise, the lady won't get killed. Oh, and mister we know about your Jet Li gunk-fu crap so don't even try. Nod up and down if you understand."

Zephrin just nodded. How would they know about me?

"See, even foreigners understand the international language," as he gestured with the gun.

"You tell'm Dave."

"Yes, Terry, that's next. Now, I do so apologize but, as I said, we forgot our Red Kettle, so, we'll have to take the ladies purse and watch, along with your wallet and watch. That pinky ring will make your donation rather special. Now, Terry, you collect the lady's purse, watch and jewelry. Sam, you collect from her gentleman friend. I'll keep the gun on them, so Hong Kong Fuey doesn't try anything."

Zephrin, just looked at the thug who spoke, saying nothing. He saw Brielle take an action that was very surprising. As Terry reached to pull Brielle closer to him, instead of resisting, she tossed her purse at him. When Terry reached to catch it, Brielle slammed her left hand into Terry's throat. Her right hand, with her fingers straight out, into his face. Blood spurted from his face as he dropped to his knees. Sam and Dave were distracted. Zephrin did a round house kick and connected to Sam's head. A resounding crunch was heard from the blow, as Sam fell to the ground like a sack of potatoes. Dave looked at his partner, lying on the ground, blood coming from where the blow had landed. Zephrin took two quick steps and then jumped at Dave. His foot connected with Dave's nose, breaking it, and driving that bone into his brain. Zephrin then saw Brielle and the thug who had attacked her. He was on the ground, his hands over his face as blood was oozing out between his fingers. Brielle was on her knees, throwing up.

Zephrin took out his phone and called 911.

"Captain Thompkins isn't going to like this," Zephrin said.

From a small grassy knoll, Laurent had watched the whole thing, through some military binoculars, while smiling.

Very impressive, mon ami. Colonel Ivano, your reputation isn't exaggerated, and you eliminated my loose ends at the same time. I'm sure we'll get better acquainted in the future. For now, I've a few plans to make and Captain

Thompkins will spend some time with you, so I won't have to look over my shoulder.

The police and two ambulances arrived about ten minutes later. The thug hit his head against the curb when he fell and was unconscious.

"Brielle, where did you learn to do that?" he asked.

"Oh, with my fingers or the purse?"

"Both."

"My brother taught that to me. He wanted me to know some self-defense, for times just like this. I just never thought I'd have to use it."

The detectives spoke with them for about a half hour and the EMT's checked them out before they were taken to the station. Chuck Thompson came into the interview room, placing a cup of coffee on the table for Zephrin.

"You go from investigating a missing person, who Ms. Chalmers now says is no longer missing, to killing three thugs. Yes, in self-defense. They attempted to rob you. Well, Ms. Chalmers' story corroborates yours. The three dead thugs were ID'd as petty criminals from the Wooster area. That is rather impressive, killing three thugs, two with knives and one with a gun."

"Three? Only the two I fought were dead when the medics arrived."

"Yes, but the third one died at the hospital. Seems that her fingernails did more than poke his eyes out. They penetrated the back of the eye socket and went into the brain," as he briefly shivered. "You mean that Ms. Chalmers killed him?" Zephrin asked.

"Yes, but it was self-defense. It's late and I see no reason to keep you both here. You two can go now. Since you've arrived, I've been quite busy. There have been four dead bodies to deal with."

"Four?" Zephrin asked.

"Yes, they found a chewed-up body, out at Funk Bottoms, the day after you arrived. Turns out he worked at the University, a Mike Dunbar. I don't believe in coincidences, so maybe there's a connection that I'm not worldly enough to know."

"Captain Thompson, Ms. Chalmers informed me earlier today, that she'd had a call three or four days ago that she was sure came from Ms. d'Estange. The caller informed her that she had to return to Sofia, Bulgaria to attend her sister's funeral and take care of the estate. Ms. d'Estange has no sister, or least none her daughter informed me of. Also, if she had returned to Sofia, why hasn't she had any contact with her daughter?"

"Some very valid points and as strange as this sounds, I agree with you. Our research also shows no record of Agate d'Estange having a sister. So far you haven't done anything illegal. Make sure you keep it that way. Please, do enjoy the rest of this evening and, Colonel, there had better not be any more dead bodies, capisci?"

After they had left, Cecil asked. "Why did you let him go? You could've held him for at least two days."

"You're right, I could have held him. His first call would be to his client, who'd call the Bulgarian UN ambassador who would call the State Department or the Bulgarian Ambassador who'd then call State. I don't need that headache right now. However, we'll have him tailed for a day or so. Don't need to be overly secretive, just making sure he behaves."

CHAPTER 10

Ashland, Ohio

Zephrin saw Brielle to her house. A small, old Levitt Cape Cod fully restored. One floor, green with light blue shutters. The front porch was screened in and had a small couch swing, table, and chairs. There were two hanging baskets of Mum's and the front flower bed was empty, waiting for next spring. Zephrin said, "You've an exceptionally fine house, Brielle. Did you do this by yourself?"

"The decorating and limited landscaping, yes. When I found the house, it needed work. My brother came to look at it, explained what needed to be done, helped me buy it for a good price. I worked with the contractors, to get it back in shape."

"Well, it's late and I've got to drive back to my hotel in Cleveland."

"Nonsense. Please, Zephrin, I don't want to be alone right now, not after the night we had. The least I can do is offer you a couch. Before you protest, it's not an imposition or an inconvenience, nor does my brother live nearby. Besides, I'm scared."

"You were very brave tonight and I do understand being scared. I'll accept your hospitality, Brielle."

"Thank you, I'll get a few blankets and a pillow and then I'll make us a pizza. Would you like a beer or something else to drink?"

"You wouldn't happen to have a red Litu Lazio, would you?"

"No, but I do have a Castle Rock Mendocino Pinot Noir."

With a sigh he replied, "It'll do. You say that your brother taught you what you did against that thug?"

"Yeah. Our parents died when I was seven. Timothy, he's chief surgeon at a hospital in Bismarck, he taught me the judo our parents taught him. Oh, they tried to teach me when I was younger, but I wasn't into it. They taught Tim. I have a sister and brother-in-law in Wyoming and Tim also taught her a few moves."

Later that night, while on the porch, Zephrin called his mother, speaking in Bulgarian.

"Mother, I've news about Agate and we have a problem."

"Problem?"

"I'll get to that, but first, Agate. Baba is going feral. Someone who works at the University with Agate, was murdered and I and a friend and fellow professor friend of Agate, Brielle, were attacked by some thugs. They're dead and we're not hurt. Brielle said she had a phone call from Agate three or four days ago, saying that Agate had to go back to Sofia for a funeral. The local police know so they may well be calling you. Now, is it possible that Baba has a sister you didn't know about?"

There was a long pause from Talrya.

"Why do you ask?"

"The funeral that Agate told her about, was for that of her sister."

"Really? No, Zephy, she has no sister, though there are a few women that she thought of as sisters. None of them live in Sofia. Did she give a name?"

"No and another thing, when Brielle and I were attacked by those thugs, she used what I think is a Draco Vydra move, Fang Strike, the distraction was good, the slash, and then her straight fingers to the eyes."

"That is an old move and one Agate knew, along with at least fifty or so others. It's become popular in self-defense classes. Sometimes the fingers are replaced with car keys."

"Thought so. Also, check on any vampires in Bismarck, North Dakota for me. That's where Brielle's brother, Timothy, lives. He taught her that move. Also, check on the name of Chalmers, that's her last name. One last check. Have someone with some pull, contact Al-Jazeera America and see if they can speak to Laurent Fortesque. I need to know if he's there or not. If they can't speak with him, I'd bet he's had word of Agate and is also looking for her."

Chuck Thompson was reading the e-mail, for the third time, out loud to Zarkof Tashkent.

***

Captain Thompson,

My name is Rabbi Andrew Tazerman of Temple B'Nai. We were greatly saddened to learn of the recent death of the nephew of one of our members, Mike Dunbar. I'm requesting that you refrain from any ongoing autopsies, in accordance with our religious tradition. We'll have a representative there tomorrow to claim the body and return it home for burial. Thank you and may God bless you.

Sincerely,

Rabbi A. Tazerman

***

"Well, what do you think? Just a coincidence?"

"I can tell you he was circumcised. You don't think Mr. Dunbar was Jewish?"

"Nope. Dunbar isn't a Jewish name. Too many coincidences about this. The equation just doesn't add up.

Even if he were, I'd find that very convenient. Did you find anything else out?"

"The toxicology report showed a little alcohol and some ferrous sulfate. That coincides with Mr. Dunbar being anemic. There was a partial six pack of beer at the camp, so that explains the low blood alcohol. Ferrous sulphate and B-12 were found at his house, both are common treatments for anemia. His blood type was O positive. His WBC was remarkably high. Oh, one other item of note. I'm still of the opinion, the bite in Mike's neck was a human bite, based on its size."

"That's repulsive! A human bite? Thanks, I'll get a BOLO ready for everyone to start looking for Count Dracula." Chuck then called Cecil.

"That's about as good a joke as you've had this year, Chuck," said Zarkof.

"Hey Cecil, when you were checking Dunbar's place out, did you find anything to suggest that he was Jewish?"

"There was a menorah by the door into the kitchen."

With a sigh, Chuck replied, "Thanks. Oh, and knowing how much you just love coincidences, I think I found another one. It's possible that our international man of adventure might-- and I mean might-- be Agate's grandson."

"What do you mean, might be?"

"I found this Zephrin Ivano easily enough. Stuff we already know. Passport information, his ISIA information lists him as a special investigator. Weapons permits, all in order. He's an Italian citizen, it was earned through service in the San Marco Marines Regiment. Upon leaving the marines, he joined the Carabinieri. My research about Talrya Nekos, indicates that she has a son, with the same first name. I found it while doing a search of Bulgarian newborns whose mothers name was Talrya. The name of a boy, Zephrin, came up. No date of birth or last name with it."

"Okay, Cecil, let's say he is. Why lie about it?"

"Don't know. Maybe disowned by daddy, could be a black sheep or bastard. Maybe Sebastian Cole II, the owner of SeCo Mining, doesn't know about Zephrin."

Wooster, Ohio

"Jania, it's a pleasure to meet you," Laurent said. "Welcome to Wooster, Ohio, the capital of boredom and drudgery. The place has a pool, though closed for the season, cable, and a nearby ice machine. All the amenities of home if you're a peasant. I hope it wasn't any inconvenience for you to get here so quickly?"

Jania was a seeker for the Traditionalists. Find vampires and record all that you can about them. She was especially good at it. Standing in at a tad over 5 feet tall and 105lbs, dripping wet, brown hair dyed purple and dressed goth a style Laurent didn't like. He felt it Americanized the

Victorian Mourning Dress she was wearing. Yet style wasn't why he accepted her.

"No, Laurent, I'm glad to help. What do you want me to do? I've heard that you might have a problem with Zephrin."

"No problem at all. As a matter of fact, I'm in the process of making him wear out his welcome with the local police. What I want you to do is find someone for me. Going by the name of Agate d'Estange. She might also be using Henriette Tangre. Here's a picture of her. Find her, that's all. I know your penchant to prove your skill. This Agate might be developing the Fangs of Death. She's exceedingly well versed in Draco Vydra, such that I'd be wary of taking her on. Locate her so that she can be recovered for research."

"Where do I start looking for her?"

"I had some luck while searching her house. On this flash drive are several pictures of a pin map of Ohio. Those red pins on it might represent places she's visited. Analyze and investigate. You have my number if you need to contact me."

"Wouldn't giving me the map have been easier?"

"Yes, but its absence might be noticed, not by these locals but by one or two others and I'd like to keep my presence unknown to them."

"Can I bring in a team once I've located her? If she suspects when I find her, she might run, and I'd waste more time searching."

Laurent thought about this, it's pros and cons.

"Sure. Looking for your grandmother who has 'mental' issues and walks away from home. Yet, the police might hear and look as well... and that might not me a bad thing, you look for Henriette Tangre."

CHAPTER 11

Warsaw, Poland: The Marie Curie Institute, Warsaw

Dr. Maven West, Director of Medical Research for the institute, read the note for the third time. The tears that had fallen on it, didn't ruin the message.

Mind is changing as forces collide. Seek the cave with the Devil's jump. The Prince and the bastard will meet. My flower needs to be protected. Sub Rosa will reveal the danger.

Agate Henriette

"Marie, please ask Dr. Malcolm and Lt. Colonel Garibaldi to join me, as soon as possible. It's important." Marie was the institutes A.I, patterned after Marie Curie. Whose initial research into vampires going feral, led to her tragic death, by radiation. That was the secret purpose of the Institute. To the world, they were the foremost researchers in radiation.

"Yes, Dr. West," Marie replied.

Two men entered the room a little later.

"What's up, Maven?" asked Dr. Reginald Malcolm, Director of Advanced Biophysics, for the institute.

"Henriette is in trouble. She sent her evacuate trigger and I think she's being hunted. Marie, please display Henriette's message."

They looked at the screen in the control room, now showing Agate's message.

"What does the part about –My flower needs to be protected -mean, Maven? I don't recognize it," said Reginald.

"I'm not sure... you're right, William, it's not part of her trigger. It probably refers to her grandson, Zephrin Ivano."

"What does Sub Rosa mean; I know the translation, literally 'Under the Rose.'"

"Reggi, it implies that something secret is hidden, someplace."

"Thanks, Bill."

Colonel Garibaldi, the institute's Director of Security, replied. "Where is she and who's tracking her?"

Dr. West looked at Dr. Malcolm, who just nodded.

"Since she sent the trigger message, Agate Henriette believes she is going feral. The being tracked part would be by her bastard grandson, Laurent Fortesque, a Traditionalist. Zephrin Ivano would also be looking for her, at the request of Agate's daughter, Talrya Nekos. Now, to complicate things, Laurent doesn't know of his relationship to Agate or Talrya and neither does Zephrin."

The Colonel's eyes widened, and his mouth opened ever so slightly. "But how and why was that hidden from him?"

"If you need to know, you'll be told," said Dr. Malcolm.

"Colonel," Maven said. "We need to get Agate out before those two men meet. She is one of our original founders and my sister. She has provided us with a large amount of our backing. If Laurent and Zephrin meet, another vampire war could start and that is something we must avoid, at all costs. I know our resources in America are extremely limited. She does have a tracking device, one of our newer models."

"Okay doc, I'll go get her. Just let me know where she is and how close either of those two might be. Okay, now one question. You've told me why I'll be getting Agate out, now why before Laurent and Zephrin meet?"

Maven West looked at Colonel Garibaldi. "Okay, how well do you follow genealogy?"

"Generally, I stop at cousin and don't worry about firsts, seconds and removed."

"Okay, Agate is the niece of Vlad Draculea, Prince of Wallachia and Head of the House Draculesti. Now for the complicated part, Laurent is the elder, so he could inherit the title, Prince of Wallachia, if recognized by Talyra or the Council of Princes. If that happens, then on his 150th birthday, he will become a member of the Council of Princes, two things that must never be allowed to happen. Now, the one saving grace is that he doesn't know of that relationship to present his claim. If they meet, they'll fight and a fifty-fifty of Zephrin dying, is something either wouldn't like."

"Maybe sometimes I'll learn not to ask too many questions."

"Good, we'll get a packet together and you can bring two others with you. You'll cross the border from Canada. Then head to a place in Ohio. That's the pickup point. We've no idea how close any of those following her are. You and your team should be ready in three hours."

"You got it. Besides myself, I'll bring Angela Simons and Larry Sherwood."

Ashland, Ohio

As he came in from the porch, he noticed the pleasurable smell of tomatoes, basil and parsley with a hint of olive oil. He went into the kitchen, Brielle, her red tinted, brown hair, looked at home stirring a pot on the stove.

"You're making the sauce for the pizza?"

"Why, yes, I am. Did your nose or eyes tell you first?"

"The aroma of fresh cooked food just warms a kitchen up, like no prepackaged product can do."

"Eat well, laugh often, love much," Brielle replied.

"As it should be," Zephrin returned, to which Brielle just smiled and nodded.

"Are you doing okay, after what happened earlier?"

Brielle stopped mixing the sauce and sighed. "I've never killed anyone before…It's unnerving, sickening. The blood and brains were all over my hand. I thought they would never come off. It still feels like my hand is covered with that…that gunk," as she shivered.

"Is it like this a lot in your line of work? Was it the same for you?"

Zephrin put his hands lightly on her shoulders.

"Yes, it was, Brielle. Do you know what those I've killed shared with the one you killed?"

"No," she said softly.

"They were criminals and murderers. If you hadn't killed him, he'd have raped you and then killed you or beat you. Now, where is that wine you mentioned? If you get a couple of glasses, I'll pour."

They spent the next hour talking, while polishing off the pizza and the bottle of wine. As she was getting some blankets for Zephrin to use on the couch, she commented,

"I saw the way you looked at Agate's paintings. Do you like her work?"

"Very much so, the European influence is there and yet, there's a difference." Zephrin knew he was lying. He couldn't tell her of his relationship with Agate. He'd done it so many times and for so many years, he just did it, with hardly any thought. Yet tonight, for the first time in a long time, he had regret.

"Would you like to see another one? She gave me one, as a present for my attaining tenure in March of this year. Marked it "DON'T OPEN TILL YOUR BIRTHDAY" I haven't even looked at it yet."

"Sure, I'd love to see it and when is your birthday?"

"Great, we'll both be the first to look at it. It's in the attic.

"You put an unopened painting in the attic, without even peeking at it?"

"Yes, Agate means it when she tells you what to do. She'd have known if I peeked and that would've disappointed her. I'm not sure which room to place it. I'd rather wait till I had the right place to hang it, than hang it in the wrong place. Besides, my birthday is in three months."

She knew then what was happening and gave her the present. Why? This could be an interesting painting.

It took about ten minutes to get the heat sealed and brown paper wrapped picture, down to the living room. When unwrapped, the two of them just looked in surprise at the painting. It showed a priest, behind an altar or table, a large silver chalice with a dusty gold base on the table. There were eight people around the altar, yet none of their faces were visible. One figure was holding an open book as if the priest were reading from it. The priest was holding crossed swords, yet the stunning part of the picture was the priest's face. It was Zephrin's.

A block away was a police car, with two officers, who'd, been following Zephrin.

"Clark, radio the chief that Zephrin didn't return to Cleveland, it looks like he'll be spending the night with Ms. Chalmers."

Sofia, Bulgaria

At the CEO's office of SeCo Mining, a rather attractive red-haired woman entered, briskly. She closed the door just under what most would consider slamming. The man behind the desk, Sebastian Cole, CEO of SeCo, was gazing out the window. He turned as she entered.

"Why Talrya, dear, you know I really like that perfume. However, it doesn't match the look on your face or the furry with which you closed the door. There's a problem I'm sure and I hope it's not me. I also think you might have added a freckle, did you devour any souls recently?"

"No Sebastian, it's not you, though adding another freckle after that comment is an interesting thought. My concern is Agate and Zephy."

"What do you mean?"

"I'm not sure. I hired Zephy to go to America and check on Agate. She had missed two of our weekly calls when I asked him. Now it's three. Zephy called me last night and asked if she might have a sister I didn't know about and agreed that Agate has the Fangs of Death. One of Agate's coworkers had been murdered along with three thugs who attacked Zephy."

"Dear, I've asked you many times before, not to call our son Zephy. At over one hundred and seventeen years of age, it's rather inappropriate. Zephrin can handle himself, very well I'll add, so why the concern?"

"Laurent Fortesque may also be looking for Agate."

"I see. I'll make some calls; why don't we have your favorite for dinner, and you can fill me in on what you haven't told me."

Ashland, Ohio

"Zephrin, how is this possible? That's your face as the priest, no not a priest; you're dressed as a Cardinal."

"Excellent observation, the raiment, is that of a Cardinal. Cardinals elect the Pope and are sometimes called the Princes of the Church. As for how.... well...huh, you see, that... err, my client is Agate's daughter, but she is also my mother. That makes Agate, my grandmother."

Brielle's face was seething in anger. Her eyes were rapidly moving from the painting to him. Her arms now folded across her chest.

"You're a fucking jerk! Excuse my French, but why didn't you tell me this before? What, you didn't think that would be important? Wait just one minute; you kept that a secret on purpose! It's obvious that there's more to what's going on but I'm sure it's family business. Is that why those thugs tried to rob us? You almost got me killed! So, you're the little boy in her paintings. You're an ass hole!"

She slapped him across the face, her fingernail making a small cut on his right ear. Zephrin was surprised by the force of her blow. The sight, or maybe the realization of what she'd done, brought her back.

"Oh my God, Zephrin, I'm sorry. I mean I'm pissed but slapping you was not what I wanted, I overreacted." Brielle got a tissue from her pocket and dabbed the small amount of blood up. Her face grimacing with emotions as her eyes welled up and a few tears came out, as she started to cry.

"No need to apologize, Brielle, you have every right to be angry at me. Though remind me that getting you mad, and pissed off, is a bad thing to do. I lied to you, though I didn't want to. It's just part of my job. I'm deeply sorry I did and yes, there's more, but I can't tell you right now. Maybe later, we'll see how things go with my investigation. I know that you've had a really bad day and this information was a shock. Now, as for why I'm the face of the Cardinal? I've no clue. But maybe the painting itself can tell us?"

He used a napkin to wipe her tears away.

"Okay, but please don't lie to me again. So, are you an undercover Cardinal for the Church? Should I beware the Spanish Inquisition?" she asked with a smile.

"Hardly, I'd never pass the requirements to become ordained; you know chastity, belief in God and a few others. This is a different type of painting than Agate usually does. No country setting, no buildings, not even pastels colors. She used bold, dark colors and it's an indoor picture."

"You mean that you're not chaste? As for the actual painting, those are good observations. I'll add she used watercolors, good ones but not the oils she normally uses. She didn't sign it and it looks like she painted from the outside in, instead of the inside out."

"Are those details important?"

"Yes, they are. I've never seen a painting Agate did in this manner. Painters rarely change their styles; it's like a fingerprint. If she hadn't given me this painting, I'd never guess that she made it. As a matter of fact, this is like a painting by Rembrandt, The Conspiracy of Claudius Civilis. Yet there are noticeable differences. The chalice is on the altar, not being held. Your image is holding crossed swords, along with the fact that everyone's face is hidden, either their back is to us or hoods cover them, except the Cardinal's. The hooded figure holding an open bible, so that the Cardinal can read it, has been added. It has thin fingers and a wedding ring; I'd say the figure is a woman. Otherwise the coloring and setting is the same. All the people are wearing mixed clothes, well made, but simple."

"Brielle, I'm not sure it's a bible. You can't see very much of the book. Granted it's being held open as if he could read it. The book itself has nothing distinguishing about it. Don't assume it's a bible because the figure is a Cardinal. I notice things, it goes with being a detective, and you know art. I'll tell you what I see, and you can let me know if it has any meaning in art or for Agate."

Mansfield, Ohio

Jania Mikos was on the bed, a box with a half-eaten pizza, along with an empty container of wings, by her side. Her laptop was on a stand. She was sucking the contents of a plastic tube, J.D. Majors Intense flavored yogurt, Cherry Red. There were four empty tubes in the trash. "Now, where would an old lady vampire hide if she was going senile?"

Her fingers played the keys like a child using a clacker paddle toy.

"Shit, no matches again, I've been at this for two days and no results. I've checked all the sites on the map, and nothing lines up. I know there's a pattern, I just need a key. Okay, must be looking at it the wrong way. Laurent says this lady is a smart, tough vampire. She'd have to figure the map would be seen. It was hanging in plain sight, for anyone to see, so she must have wanted someone to see it, but who? Zephrin, that's who, she might have left a message for him in this. Okay, what do I see in the picture? Red pins with green and white yarn, all radiating from Ashland. No, wait, they don't all radiate from Ashland, some connect to other pins. Could be a travel log perhaps? Okay, time for some editing."

Ashland, Ohio

Zarkhof was finishing his paperwork when his computer dinged. That indicated an answer to an inquiry he made. He opened the email from an associate, Robin Meyers, the M.E. in Akron, Ohio. She had a double murder where one of the victims was anemic.

He sent back a reply to Robin. "I've run a full blood work up on my victim and I'd like you to do the same and we'll compare our results. Oh, one other question, what can you let me know about the two murder victims? Thanks, Zarkhof."

***

While Brielle went back into the kitchen, to dispose of a few pieces of crust and rinse the empty bottle and glasses. Zephrin was looking at the magazines on the coffee table. He saw a smaller newspaper, The Collegian, the University newspaper, dated two days ago. Pulling it from under the magazines and stone block pizza board, he saw a picture of Laurent Fortesque and whistled.

"Whistling when your happy, Zephrin?" Brielle said from the kitchen.

"Close, I was looking at the university newspaper and saw that the Director of Al-Jazeera America visited the campus."

"Oh, yes he did. It was a big deal. He contacted the University President about doing an article for Al-Jazeera and came out. Met with the Muslim students on campus, gave a speech and all. As a matter of fact, one of my, well Agate's students, helped give him a tour of the campus, he left the next day, yesterday."

"What was he here for, I mean, what was the article about?"

"Something about young Muslim students and how they integrate into and with American culture. Read the write up the paper did."

Zephrin did as asked. The article wasn't bad. There were several quotes from Laurent about terrorism and suicide bombers, being reactionary elements expressing their frustration with the political situation. This demonstrated their weak minds by not understanding the result of their actions. The students, for the most part, didn't endorse or support the terrorist's actions. They talked about their friends here and that they feel accepted by their fellow students. Several mentioned that they had dated outside of their faith. Well I didn't expect a smoking gun, but this does look legit. Still, the reason for this visit was Agate. That means he knew about me and sent those thugs after us, how else would they know about my 'kung fu?' This changes things dramatically, and Brielle is at risk.

CHAPTER 12

Denver, Colorado

Dr. Javier Daniels, CEO of San Guine Pharmaceuticals, was on video conference with the American Vampire Council. The five most senior vampires in America; Asbeel, Penemue, Kasdaye, Gadreel and Yeqon. These five individuals were always known by one of these five names, not the ones they had when elected. That was the tradition of the American Vampire Council.

"Yes, Asbeel, I understand your concerns, but this is a higher chance than I'd like to take, now that Zephrin's involved. Accidents happen and we've had skirmishes in the past."

"Javier," Kasdaye replied. "Yes, we've had our skirmishes and accidents have happened. More than either side will admit but never with one of such rank. Don't forget that his parents are the owner and head geologist at SeCo. His mother is the stepdaughter of their current leader, Alu-Card. They have immense pull and influence in Europe and the UN. His death, however 'accidental' it looked, could start a second civil war. You do know about how the first one went."

Yeqon added, "The humans called it the 100 Years War. I lost my great aunt, Jeanneton Darc. Over one million seven hundred and fifty thousand humans died. So did almost sixteen thousand vampires. We still haven't recovered from those losses. The humans have and then some."

"You see how much of a problem that would become?" Penemue asked.

"How many of us would die in a modern war? Neither us nor the Modernists like each other, but protecting our existence is always paramount," added Gadreel.

"Zephrin is a full-blooded vampire Prince, descended from Vlad Draculea and heir to the titular leadership of the Council of Princes'. Thus, this council, in a unanimous decision, denies your request for war as well as Zephrin's death," said Kasdaye.

Asbeel looked at the other two, then back at Javier, "You do understand the directives you've been given?"

With a sigh, Javier looked at the five of them and said "Yes." Then he ended the video conference. His assistant came in, as if on cue.

"Conference didn't go as planned, sir?"

"No, Anthony, it didn't. I'm not sure what to do next. If I don't follow my instructions, our pentagonal council will be terribly upset."

"Well sir, that's true, provided it's still a pentagon, if I understand my politics correctly."

With widened eyes, Jeremiah smiled. "Why Anthony, you might have a point. I'll need the organizational papers of the American Vampire Council."

"They're already on your computer, sir. A recent upgrade. I'm sure."

Ashland, Ohio

Brielle returned, setting two clean glasses down.

"Okay, new wine, clean glasses, and no more lies. I'm trying to help you, Zephrin. This is a Niagara, what do you think the crossed swords mean?"

"I'll do my best to not lie to you. Sometimes lying is a part of my job. Most of the time I do it without a second thought. Yes, I can tell you really do want to help. As for the crossed swords, that's called saltire. They have different meanings if pointed up or down. If up, that implies ready for a fight. The French term en garde was meant as a warning to fight before guns became the main weapon."

"Well, it would seem that, as a detective, being ready to fight is a job requirement."

"It is, but I'm also in the Italian Carabinieri; we're our own branch of the military with national policing responsibility."

"Well, the military does fight. What about the meaning of the chalice?"

"Well that could reference the Last Supper and Communion, blood being shed, sacrifice. Drinking from the same chalice could mean agreement, bonding, sharing. The chalice is of two parts. A new shiny silver cup part and the old, dirty, tarnished base made of brass."

"Brass looks like gold. Does that mean anything?"

"Gold doesn't tarnish, brass does but shiny brass can look like gold. It could mean rebuilding, new over the old, revolution, change, just to name a few."

"If the book isn't a bible, what book could it be?"

"I see nothing, no writing or parts of pictures, on the cover or binding."

Brielle got up and retrieved a magnifying glass from a desk, to examine the book more closely.

"I'll check the book and chalice, as they are front and center in the painting, a very important location."

"The book is just that, a blank book." After about five minutes, Brielle said, "Zephrin, it looks like something is written on the base of the chalice. I see lines that almost look like a word but not in a language I know. Here, you look."

Zephrin looked at the chalice base closely and yes, the lines were hidden in the tarnish cracks, did seem to make words.

"Brielle, could you get some paper and a pen, please?"

He began writing words down and ended up with a string of Nordic letters, that spelled the French word, "Tsiganes"

"That means Gypsy, in French," Brielle said.

"If you're looking for meaning, some say Gypsies stole the nail meant for the heart of Jesus. God rewarded them with the right to steal and that gives them a deserved reputation as thieves, con artists, hucksters and such."

***

Zarkhof was in his lab, going over the blood he had drawn before he received the request to stop.

"Now this is interesting. Mr. Dunbar was indeed anemic, leukemia even, but with a very unusual and almost unnoticeable difference. His white blood cells were mature cells, and they have the AB antigens. The red blood cells have no antigens on them. Theoretically, that could make him both a universal donor and universal recipient, at the same time, which is virtually impossible. I'd better run the tests again, just to verify these results. Mr. Dunbar's bone marrow produced mature white blood cells, not immature, like in all other cases. Mr. Dunbar had a form of leukemia that I've never heard of. Unless looking for it, blood tests would only total white vs. red cells and then label it as anemia and or leukemia. As a matter of fact, Mr. Dunbar was both. I need to save these results for further study."

Belleuve, Ohio

"Okay Charlie, your turn to check the wild caves area, off of Devil's Leap," said Rudy.

"But Rudy, I did it last month."

"True, but you lost the bet on the game Sunday, so time to pay up. See you in six hours or so, loser."

"Damn Browns." Charlie said as Rudy walked away.

Checking the Wild Caves area meant spelunking down from Devil's Leap. Looking for trash and personal effects that people might have tossed or lost. Checking for any changes in the rock formations and any new cracks or features. His helmet was equipped with both a camera and two side mounted lights.

Charlie went over to Devil's Leap and checked his gear. "Head lamp: working, camera: working, rope ladder is secure and safely attached, pitons, hammer and harness; all check." He then climbed down the rope ladder, to a ledge with a recessed area. This was the main area for anything dropped from above. Charlie began checking the area and saw a pile of rocks in the recessed section, neatly stacked in an oblong shape. Charlie was familiar enough with rocks and how they look and can fall to see that this pile wasn't random.

"Let's see, a baseball cap, the Reds, a pair of glasses, a lighter and two of the cavern's brochures. "Now what the hell is a pile of rocks doing here?" He scanned the small, recessed area, about 4 feet high and eight across. It went back about twenty feet. "No other piles, but the scattered rocks I'd expect to see are missing…or someone somehow is playing a joke on me. Rudy! He's trying to set me up. He knew I lost and could easily have gotten down here one night and did this. Okay, I'll play along and see if I can reverse it back on him."

He got down and started moving the rocks and saw the head of an elderly lady, deathly pale, eyes closed. Charlie almost fell when he saw the head. Granted he expected something but not such a realistic head and an attached body.

"Holy Shit! A body! How the hell did Rudy get a dead body down here?"

He stood up, though still stooping and began walking toward the shaft, as he thought about what to do.

"Let me see, how do I…."

Charlie was interrupted as he was grabbed on the shoulder by a pale hand and spun around. He was looking at the head he'd just uncovered, the body attached to it.

Agate looked at the human who'd disturbed her hiding spot.

"All vampires say a young human taste like chicken. I say they taste like veal."

Her mouth opened, revealing fangs as she bit Charlie's neck. His screams died in a gurgle and his echoes were hardly heard.

Once she finished her meal, Agate looked at her leftovers, noticed his name tag and shook her head. She was oblivious to the blood on her clothes. "Sorry, Charlie. However, now what do I do with you and then me?"

She picked Charlie's body up and climbed up the rope ladder about five feet or so and then mashed his neck, where she'd bitten him, against a protruding rock. Then back down to the ledge, where she had killed him. She held his body and dropped him, face first, into the blood-mud and then just kicked it off the ledge, headfirst. It took about a minute, but she heard a splash. She smashed his helmet on the ledge tossing it down. She then climbed down the rope to the Ole Mist'ry River and swam to the river room, where she meditated for a half hour before beginning her search for a new hiding place.

CHAPTER 13

Zarkhof came into Chief Thompkins's office. "Chuck, do you have a little time? It's about Dunbar's murder."

"Sure, Hans, have a seat. What's up?"

"Well, I ran a standard blood type and did a full work-up on Mr. Dunbar, standard procedure. I did this twice. I've done nothing with the body since, but I want to. The blood that was drawn is different than any anemic blood I've ever examined. Mike Dunbar was anemic; he had a verified prescription of B vitamins, a standard treatment. The results I got were very unusual, so I ran them again, with the same results. Mike Dunbar was anemic, but he also had leukemia. I don't even know if I want to call what he had leukemia, though technically, that's a correct description."

"I'm no doctor but how can you have leukemia and yet not have it?"

"His white blood cells were mature, that means they were good white blood cells. In normal leukemia, the white blood cells are immature and useless to the body's immune system. White blood cells help protect the human body from infection as well as other foreign materials. White blood cells develop and are produced in bone marrow. The lack of white blood cells or the incidence of too many can cause serious disorders in the body. A common disorder from a lack of white blood cells is called leukopenia. A person is more susceptible to infections and contagious diseases. Mike's blood type was AB. He also might have been something I've never heard of, a universal donor and recipient for blood transfusions."

"Never heard of doesn't mean doesn't exist."

"True, but a possible cause of this could be radiation exposure. I found one possible case on record. Marie Curie, who died in a sanitarium in Paris in 1934 of aplastic anemia, brought about by exposure to radiation. Her white blood cells were recorded as undamaged. The AB blood type is the universal recipient. I've never seen any information that anemics are more prone to this blood type than non-anemic. Red blood cells have antigens on them, which is why we must match donors to recipients. Type O red blood cells don't have them, hence the universal recipient. Mr. Dunbar's white blood cells have the AB antigens…I've never heard of that before."

"So, you're suggesting that Mike Dunbar was exposed to radiation?"

"I seriously doubt it. Radiation sources are well known, documented, and controlled. I did send out a request to my fellow M.E.'s to see if they'd ever had such a case of anemia. Did they think that radiation could cause the AB antigen forming on the white blood cells. For me to determine if it was exposure to radiation, I'd need to examine his bone marrow. I could use a dosimeter, any blood test wouldn't work because we check for a drop in the white blood cell count, and Mike's would be abnormally higher due to his mutated anemia. I was informed by an associate, Robin Meyers in Akron, that she recently had a double murder, where one of the victims was anemic. She was running the blood work and will let me know the results for leukemia. She also told me that they had received a stop autopsy request from a synagogue in Montana. She'll forward me the results but that will take a day or two. How much do you really believe in coincidences?"

"You know I don't so what are you suggesting, a serial killer who targets anemics who also suffer from leukemia?"

"Chuck, really? Just look at the picture, a Jewish synagogue in Montana sends an e-mail, to have both autopsies stopped and will pick up the bodies. Both of which are anemic and might have a rare white blood cell condition, almost identical to leukemia. Next set of coincidences. An international detective agency comes to investigate a missing person, who's file was accidentally erased and whom now, might not be missing. Don't you think that's a lot of unrelated coincidences…or are they?"

"Valid concerns, I'll see that we check on the Synagogue in Helena, Montana. You let me know about the blood work and I'll make a call to the Akron Police and follow up with our visiting detective."

***

Jania smiled as she had made some sense of the map, though it had taken three days.

Three white pins were located at Toledo, Akron, and Columbus. Three dark green pins were at Mansfield, Dayton, and Corning. Three light green pins at Belmont, Meigs and Tiffin. Each one of the colors formed a triskelion. Combined, they didn't seem to form anything. So, Jania began checking on the pins, the center of each triskelion and any intersection points they shared.

CHAPTER 14

The Windsor Tunnel border crossing, into the United States.

"Passports please," said the border guard. "What is your purpose for visiting the United States?"

They each handed the guard their passport.

"We belong to the Spelunking Club of Toronto and are going to visit a few sites and do some spelunking. That's cave exploring, in case you didn't know," Garibaldi said.

"I didn't, so thanks. Let's see here, you're William Garibaldi." As he looked at William, in the driver's seat." You must be Angela Simmons and the gentleman in the back is Larry Sherwood. Can I see your gear?"

"Sure, it's in the back," said Garibaldi.

He turned the car off and went to the back of the van, opened the door, so the guard could see their gear.

"Well, unusual but all seems in order. How long do you plan on staying in the United States?"

"About a week, sir," Garibaldi replied.

"Enjoy yourselves and be safe, thanks for visiting the United States."

"You're welcome, sir, and thank you. I hope you enjoy your day as well."

With that, Agate's rescue team from the Marie Curie Institute, crossed into the US, heading south then east and eventually hooking up with Interstate 90 east.

Ashland, Ohio

"Brielle, since you found the word hidden on the chalice, could you check to see if any anomalies are in the picture?"

"Sure, but why would she use Nordic runes to spell a French word?"

"French is a common language. Nordic runes are old. The runes are straight lines and easy to hide. Unless you are a follower of Tolkien or RPG's, I doubt very many people would notice it."

Brielle went over the painting with a magnifying glass and pen light for forty minutes and didn't find anything.

"Now, let's move that painting, so it's leaning on your soon to be bed. It'll be easier to check it."

Zephrin's eyes widened, the frame wasn't at all like the other frames of Agate's pictures at her house. Those were light, simple frames. This was wider and very ornate.

"Brielle, check the frame."

She started at the bottom left corner and went clock ways around the frame. "Okay, found a word. It's in French: Watchers. It was written under a cactus flower."

"Agate always liked flowers. The cactus flowers mean...depending on culture, attraction, or chastity. It can also mean maternal love."

Brielle continued to the upper left corner, then began going along the top. About halfway through, "Oh, man, my back and shoulders are tightening up."

"Perhaps I can give you a back rub."

"Really? Hey, I found a second word, also in French, Parables. It was under a begonia."

"Simple, means caution or danger."

Brielle said, "I wonder." She moved to examine the right side. "Just as I thought; a third word, Astronomy, under a flowering dandelion."

"The Dent-de-lion, fighting and overcoming challenges. More of a peasants flower for meaning."

Brielle stood up. "Now, let's move this painting to lie on the couch, that'll make it easier for me to check the bottom side." They moved it and Brielle continued her examination.

"Yup, a fourth word; Dreams. It was under a poppy flower."

"Sleep, dreams and the messages they provide."

Zephrin leaned over to look at the words, through the magnifying glass that Brielle was holding.

"Why, that's great, Brielle," and he leaned into her and gave her a kiss, which she returned before pulling away.

"Zephrin, slow down."

"I'm sorry, Brielle, I didn't…"

"I was surprised, Zephrin, not offended. Though, I've rarely seen such shades of red in a person's face. Here," as she leaned in, kissing him again, her lips parted as her tongue invited his in. "Now, wasn't that better?"

"Yes."

"I would assume that those words mean something to you, by that reaction."

"Not yet, but they will. In the morning, I'm going back to Agate's house. She left these clues so there might be some I missed, care to join me?"

"Okay. Now for that back rub you promised and—well whatever happens, you're still sleeping on the couch, alone."

Zephrin didn't sleep well. A strange couch, in a strange house, in a strange city. Noises he wasn't used to. He woke up hearing Brielle crying softly, then she took a shower at 4 am. He walked upstairs and heard her saying "…got to get it off! Why won't it come off?"

Helena, Montana

Andrew Tazerman, Rabbi of Temple B'Nai, in Helena, Montana, was in his office, discussing a situation. Like most situations, it was totally unexpected, which made it especially important.

"You three are my sight, hearing, and voice. I find it interesting that the Ashland, Ohio police department and the Akron, Ohio medical examiner, have been checking out the temple website. They are also conducting searches about Mike Dunbar and Jay Syne. Yet, none of you bothered to tell me this. Now, I'm not overly concerned about the searches. However, the function of our Temple, besides tending to those of the Jewish faith, is to recover and protect the vampire secret and our faction. If we have problems, then our members will have problems trusting us and I hate it when there are those who don't trust us. So, does anyone care to tell me why we had issues with our recovery system?"

Mira Knickerbocker, Cody Banks and Frank Gorge looked at each other and then at Andrew Tazerman.

"Sir," said Mira. "We enacted our recovery protocol, upon learning of Mike Dunbar's death. The system performed as expected. It turns out that our system is more automated than we thought. It scanned for other death reports and found one for Jay Syne. It activated a second recovery protocol for him. The system responded to both deaths since it had no input to not respond."

"Yes sir, the programming issue is my responsibility. On two aspects, the programming was incomplete. The scanning for dead members was a backup in case an incomplete entry was made. Second was not requiring an inputted name to activate a recovery protocol. Those inefficiencies are being corrected. It should take another two hours," said Frank.

"Very good, now, have we come up with a way to explain to those two agencies, Cody?"

"In the works. Mike and Jay's bios were up to date. I've sent a system reminder to all of our North American members to check that their bios are up to date by next Wednesday."

"I'm sure you all understand me when I say I don't expect this to happen again."

Denver, Colorado

Dr. Daniels, or Javier, as he was known to the group, was going over the American Vampire Council's original charter. He yelled out, "Anthony, you genius!"

"The American Vampire Council will be composed of five vampires, chosen by the heads of all the houses. If at any such time, the council does not consist of five members, it's barred from conducting any new business or decisions, but all old decisions stand, and disciplinary hearings can be conducted. A new election will be held no later than twelve months after the vacancy on the AVP council, for a new

AVP council member, to which none of the living, former members can run."

The click of a door closing, followed by, "I took the liberty of bringing you some beverage and doughnuts."

"You know that the doctor said I was pre-diabetic and need to watch my sugar."

"Really, sir? When and what doctor? You should know they are Boston Cream's, your favorite."

"Yes, they are, Anthony, and of all the things out there that I do eat, sugar is the last thing I fear. Now that I've figured out the problem, I need a problem solver and I know who can help me find one."

"Sir, just to point out that they could still put you on trial for violating a direct order."

"Yes, but that would only happen after any repercussions of my action are resolved."

CHAPTER 15

Sofia, Bulgaria

The dinner consisted of czernina, a Polish blood soup, pressed duck, and curry mee. There was a reddish-brown powder that Sebastian sprinkled on his food.

"Dear, try the cinnamon blood meal. It's a new product, from our vampire food subsidiary, about four months old, we've been shipping it for about ten days now. I sent some to Zephrin and Agate earlier."

Talrya, dipped some of her pressed duck in it, slowly chewing the duck, savoring the taste experience.

"This isn't bad, dear, maybe you could make a curry or garlic flavored versions, they'll both like it. How do you get around the restrictions about ingredients being listed?"

"It's sold as an organic, naturally flavored, whole food spice. That allows it to get around most listing requirements. Your suggestion is an excellent one. I'll see that they make some samples in the morning and have them ready for you to taste in the evening. Now, please explain why Laurent and Zephrin are BOTH looking for Agate?"

"She's missed two of our regular phone calls. I was worried. I asked him to investigate and mentioned that she might be developing the Fangs of Death."

"So, you don't know if Agate actually has this. You based sending Zephrin, a hunter of feral vampires, based on your mother missing a couple of phone calls? That wasn't a wise or practical decision. You should have gone yourself. It would have raised far fewer flags. Okay, please continue."

"In our last conversation, she was distracted. Her conversation would drift between my questions, school and talk about her pottery and her new boyfriend…Casanova. She also mentioned that she had discovered some new blood in her life."

"Talrya, many times I'm distracted during our conversations. If Agate has a new boyfriend, that's great. Her referring to him as Casanova, could just be a reference as to how much she enjoys him. Remember, that she almost married Casanova. That just might be an indication as to how much she likes him."

"Oh, I remember how much she was in love with Casanova, I never trusted him, though he seemed on the sincere side. I doubt that anyone could ever replace him in her heart. Even so, I felt that her mind was beginning to slip."

"I see how, at the ripe old age of eleven, you knew what kind of character Casanova was. It's not like Agate to miss two of your phone calls, and to talk about an old, intense lover, is so unnatural for us vampires, wouldn't you agree, dear?"

"Sebastian, stop with the sarcasm. I'm serious here."

"So am I, dear. What possessed you to ask Zephrin to check on her? Unfortunately, the wrong people know that when Zephrin goes someplace, they know why and follow. Okay, so now I understand Laurent's potential involvement, but isn't that like using a hammer to kill a fly? Just call on other days and times."

"She talked about making some pottery tea sets, with creamer and sugar cups. Agate hasn't made that type of pottery in a rather long time. As for the other, I did but no answer, so I contacted Zephrin."

"Well, I've confirmed that Laurent isn't in his office, he's out doing research for an article. I'll assume that means he's in this Ashland place. I'll let Zephrin know. A friend of mine called and told me that the American Vampire Council denied a request for war and Zephrin's death. That makes me very worried, so I've alerted all our clan and allies. I'd hate to be unprepared if any accidents start happening."

Cleveland, Ohio

Laurent checked into the hotel in Cleveland. He took a room on the 4th floor, after finding out what room his dear old college friend, Zephrin Ivano, was in. He tossed his suitcase on one bed, put a duffel bag on the floor and flopped on the second bed. He reviewed his plans about what to do next. He smiled devilishly. Picking up the phone, he called for room service. "This order is for supper. I'd like the baked chicken with peas and salt potatoes, milk, and tea. For dessert, apple pie will be fine. Deliver that in two hours. Thank you."

He turned on the TV and watched the news. He sat up as he saw a follow up report about a double murder, in Akron. One name stood out, Jay Syne. "Why you beautifully effective bitch. The satisfaction of killing you might be worth the trouble it would bring for not capturing you. Well, I just might have to settle for capturing your grandson."

He was surprised when dinner was not only on time but tasted rather good. "For infidels…no, cattle can't be infidels. Cattle are property, valuable property to be sure, but still property. Yet even gods like us need those that tend the cattle and my fellow Muslim brothers and sisters will fill that bill simply fine."

His cell phone chimed, he looked a bit surprised as, the ring was unfamiliar, then he recognized the number.

"Javier, for what do I owe the honor?"

"Laurent, you were right about Mike Dunbar, but did you know that Jay Syne was also killed?"

"I saw a news report about that, a double murder, and your point being?"

"Could he have been killed by Zephrin?"

"Nope, Agate did that as well. I told you to pull them. She's hunting her enemies and, I think she's going feral."

"Pity, so is your article done? As for my call, I need a problem solver for a job."

"Yes, and not only did it turn out well, but I satisfied my real reason for going there. I found Zephrin Ivano, verified his deadly skill and am about to bug his hotel room so I can know what he's up to. Javier, I know for a fact that you are very capable of doing any killing you need done, so why an assassin?"

"It's a political person and I'd like a very good alibi."

"Understood, I'll give you a name, Taraz Bulba. I'm not sure where he is now but his contact number is A2-671-913-7734. He'll be costly, but you can afford it."

"Thanks, and you'll figure out what's going on when you hear."

He put his cell phone on the bed, "That's what worries me about you, Javier, you're deadly, but with a limited scope. You don't understand that what to you would seem important, has much bigger implications. Not everything in your way is an obstacle to be overcome."

An hour later, Laurent called the number of another room in the hotel. No answer. Then he called the front desk.

"Front desk, how may I help you?"

"This is room 414, my good friend is in room 305, Zephrin Ivano. Our club is having a reunion and I was unable to be here. My schedule freed up some time. Do you happen to know what Mr. Ivano looks like?"

"Why, yes sir, I do."

"Great, I'm going to go out. If you don't mind, I'll give you my cell number, and if you could call me to let me know when he arrives, I'd appreciate that. I want it to be a surprise when he sees me."

"That won't be a problem at all, Mr. Fortesque, I'm happy to do that for you."

"Thank you very much."

He then opened his suitcase. Took out some thick rope, a harness, small backpack, locking clamps and an insulated, head to toe, black suit. After putting the suit on, he secured one end to the rail on his small balcony and then began lowering himself down the side of the hotel in between the balconies. He went down one floor and then jumped onto a balcony.

"These modern hotels are great. Electronic keyed locks for the doors but a quite simple latch lock for the balcony door."

He jimmied it in five seconds and entered. He proceeded about the room placing several listening devices in the main room and kitchenette area yet decided against the bedroom.

"Even I feel that some rooms are meant to be private, mon ami."

He left, locking the balcony door and returned, via the rope, to his own room.

Sofia, Bulgaria

"Sebastian, how sure are you of this information," asked the man on Sebastian's computer screen.

"Acting Prince Alu'Card, I'm completely confident that my source didn't lie to me. It's possible he was either misled or lied to."

"A request for war, to any council is of grave concern. I'll approach the American Vampire Council about this. They have no requirement or obligation to tell me anything, but I'm more likely to get a response than you are. It might take a couple of days, but I will get back to you."

CHAPTER 16

Bellevue, Ohio

"Okay Rudy, tell me again about Charlie," the Seneca County sheriff said.

"Yeah, well Uncle Alfred, um, we were doing our end of season check of the caves, making sure all was okay. I mean, you don't want any tourist garbage to be left lying around. The caves below Devil's Leap are not open to the public but sometimes they wander, and we've found stuff at the bottom. It's a pain to check it out, none of us like it. Well, ya see, Charlie lost a bet on account of the Browns losing the game, so he had to take my rotation. I'd said I'd see him in a few hours and went back."

"Did he have his safety equipment?"

"Absolutely, it's required that we check each other's equipment before we enter the caves. Charlie was a stickler for safety."

"So, you never saw him go down the line to check that area?"

"No, sir."

"Thanks, Rudy, you can go, for now."

After Rudy left, "Well, Raymond, what do you think?"

"Kid's legit, it was probably just an accident. His rope was attached to a weak rock section. The rock broke free, might have been already cracked. Charlie's weight caused it to snap, the sudden shift causing him to lose his balance and fall, hitting the wall, then landing on the ledge. He bounced off and down the shaft, into the river. We saw the pictures where he hit the cave wall on the way down and the ledge where he hit, then bounced, and continued to fall into the water. His gear made him sink to the bottom."

"Makes sense, sort of, an accidental death. OSHA might have an issue about how a stickler for safety didn't check the attachment point but otherwise, I agree with you. Let's head back and write it up but check out if he owed anyone money or had any enemies. They're retrieving the body now and then it goes to the morgue. His hat with the camera was found and is going to be examined, maybe something will be found on the camera."

Wooster, Ohio

Jamia's computer beeped. She logged in and noticed a news article. An employee at the Seneca Caverns died when doing the end of year check, fell to his death. The rock he'd attached his rope to broke free, causing him to fall.

That's in Bellevue, Ohio and is one of the pins from the map. That's it! She's hiding in a cave complex that just closed for the season, reopens at the end of April, next year, time to call my team in.

Ashland, Ohio

Zephrin and Brielle entered Agate's house. She checked the plants, windows and answering machine while Zephrin went upstairs to check the art workroom and bedroom. Everything was as he had left it, the finished paintings still there. What the hell am I missing? He walked into Agate's bedroom and flopped on his back onto her bed, staring at the ceiling. Brielle appeared in the doorway.

"Well, now I am insulted. I never felt my couch was that uncomfortable. Sleeping on the job isn't something I'd expect of an international man of mystery. By the way, did you find anything or come up with an idea? I called into the college for some time off based on what happened yesterday."

"Shh," Zephrin replied, putting a finger to his lips. "That's my secret. I do the unexpected, and I do it very well, and that's why I'm an international man of mystery. Please, don't tell anyone."

"Even if I did, they'd never believe me. I've always loved four poster beds like this. She said this bed's been in her family for over one hundred years. As she is your grandmother, is that true?"

"It just might be. I could see it being passed down. I remember it from when I was a little kid, she loved it when she saw it. The rose flowers are carved from Rosewood as the crowns on the four posts, why...Porca vacca!" as

Zephrin bolted up and stood on the bed, checking the rose carvings.

"They're called finials, Zephrin, not porca vaccas. What's up?"

Zephrin stood on the bed and began examining the rose flower finials at one of the posts.

"Sub-Rosa, my dear, it's a fancy way to say something is hidden."

He checked the second one and on the third one he smiled and pressed a thorn on a stem. The rose moved about an eighth of an inch and he moved it a little more. He reached up and found a small hole with a piece of paper in it. He pulled it out and moved the rose carving back.

He unrolled the paper and saw it was written in Bulgarian.

"Oh, a secret compartment. Is your shoe also a secret phone? What does the note say?" asked Brielle.

Zephrin looked at Brielle, "Why would my shoe be a secret phone?" He began reading the note.

'Zephy, my little Prince. Yes, it's started and though I know you, your job, and your mother very well. DON'T come looking for me. You'll get in the way and I'd rather not worry about your safety, because you couldn't stop me. Besides, I need you to do something much more important. Protect my curator from Laurent. The lamb needs you. More importantly, she's special."

"What does the note say?"

"Have a look but she wrote it in Bulgarian." He handed her the note.

"I won't lie to you, Brielle, but right now I can't tell you all of it. She doesn't want me to find her and she does want me to make sure you're okay and to protect you from someone."

Brielle handed it back, after looking at it. "You're right it's in Bulgarian. Protect me from who?"

"You can read Bulgarian?" Zephrin said, with a hint of worry. "Protect you from Laurent Fortesque, the Director of Al-Jazeera America."

"No, I don't, but she uses the same language in the Rolodex in her office. Well then, that's that. Your grandmother just leaves without telling anyone before she goes. However, she leaves cryptic hidden note about making sure I'm okay and to protect me from a glorified reporter? Zephrin, you didn't lie but you've created a whole bunch of questions. Please don't think I'm an idiot. It diminishes the person you are. I like Agate, she was the best professor I ever had, got me a job here and we were, no, are good friends. I owe her for what she's done for me. Between the thugs and painting with your image in it, I know they weren't coincidences. I've lived in Ashland for almost fifteen years. I've never been assaulted or not felt safe walking at night. So, I know there's something else going on, just like the police figure. Please tell me. I want to help find Agate, so please let me help."

With a look at the floor and then back to Brielle, Zephrin nodded.

"Okay, Brielle, you've shown how much you want to help, and I believe you and trust you. I'm not a special detective for the ISIA. I own it. I don't have much to do with its operation, that's left to the people I have in place. Now, as you know, Agate was a professor of art at Sorbonne, in Paris. About twenty years ago, before I bought it, ISIA helped Interpol capture a suspected terrorist in Paris. Agate was rather instrumental in that capture. The criminal captured was Laurent's cousin. The note she left was to tell me not to look for her and to protect someone, who I think is you. She referred to her curator and as you take care of her house, including plants and paintings. She also said that you're special to her and she doesn't want you hurt."

"You really think…" There was something in Zephrin's tone and eyes that made her stop what she was going to say. "If you say so, but I'll reserve judgment for now and hope that you wouldn't lie to me, again. You're a hard person to read and I'm exceptionally good at reading people. The best way to protect me is that we stay together, wouldn't you agree? I can tell by the look on your face, you're going to ignore her advice about stopping to look for her."

"Yes, Brielle, and thanks for understanding."

"Zephrin, I don't understand but I won't push for the full truth right now, though the international man of mystery has lost a bit of its luster. Now, so that I don't get any more upset, for what reason would Agate want you to protect me?"

"She's afraid of Laurent going after you to get to her?"

"He was on campus before I even knew, and he made no attempt to talk with me. I only knew of him being here when one of the students mentioned it. Now that I think about it, Afnan did mention that he'd asked if he could meet Agate. She told him about her going missing and that he, Laurent, had seen the two of us walking across campus one day."

"What day was that?"

"It was two, no, three days ago."

"That would make it the day before we were attacked. Which I'm now sure was arranged by Laurent and we proceeded to kill the only three witnesses that could prove it."

"I owe you an apology, Zephrin. It does indeed seem that Laurent was looking for Agate. He saw you were here and decided to eliminate us and then leave."

"Maybe not. Agate doesn't have any sisters so that was either a fake phone call or it was her just leaving a hidden clue. What do you remember about the phone call? Do you remember anything unusual or different that she said?"

"Let me think." …Brielle closed her eyes and they moved rapidly, as if she was in REM sleep, then she spoke.

"Oh, Brielle, sorry to bother you so late, but I've been on pins and needles due to the death of my sister. The whole yarn would take a lot of time, so the short version is all I've time for. She died in a car accident. A sink hole opened in the road right in front of her car. She died when her car fell into a cave so big, the devil couldn't leap across it. Would you believe that? The ambulance was called, and though they got her to the hospital, they couldn't save her."

"That was amazing, Brielle! You remembered a phone call perfectly, from three weeks ago. Yes, it does help. Agate had no sisters, so she was telling you something and now I know why she wanted me to protect you. So, you could tell me. Now, I do believe that there was a map in the hallway that had pins, needles and yarn in it."

Bellevue, Ohio

Jania arrived in Bellevue as the sun was beginning its descent for the day. She pulled into a spot in front of the Amsden House Restaurant. She walked in, two older guys talking fishing were at a table near the door. There were two others at the counter and a family was at a booth in the back. She saw a local paper, grabbed a copy, and sat a couple of tables from the door. A teenaged girl came up to her and handed her a menu.

"Evening, I'm Michelle, and if you don't mind my saying so, that's a cool outfit you have on. Would you like some coffee while you decide what you want?"

"Thanks, Michelle, coffee with sugar would be great. I'm here to visit a friend in the hospital and waiting for a couple of others to join me. They might be a while, so what would you recommend?"

"Well, it's dinner time but the trash potatoes are particularly good. Pancakes or a Reuben would be great with them. My boyfriend, who's the best cook here, is in the kitchen. You want them fully loaded?"

"Sure, sounds delicious. Breakfast for dinner, why not? A glass of O.J. would be nice as well."

"You got it, be a few minutes."

As Michelle left, Jania opened the paper and began reading. It was a terrible thing about that boy who died in the cave accident. The article referred to both the police report and M.E.'s autopsy report that no alcohol or drugs were found. The paper mentioned that Charlie was an excellent tour guide who knew the caves like the back of his hand and followed the regular safety procedures. This just gave her more reason to feel that Agate had been the cause. An experienced employee dies of a freak accident in a cave. Granted it could happen but, when you're looking for a vampire, who's on the run, simple explanations sprout from simple minds. Now, just wait for a few helpers to do the search.

Unknown Location

Taraz Bulba was listening to what the potential client wanted done; one of the American Vampire Council members killed and his family. He didn't care which one, just one of them, within the next ten days. A very ominous, though profitable contract, if accepted. Yes, could make him a wanted man, it might start a war and war is very profitable. His mind drifted back to his childhood. Dad told him of how his grandfather, The Count of Lorraine had died at the Battle of Crecy during the civil war. His chest and abdomen pierced by arrows from an English peasant's longbow, a normal human. Grandpa had fought on the wrong side. Dad rectified the problem of sides but, in the end, Dad's side lost that war. That's why Taraz never concerned himself with sides, just who paid and how much. Do I, or don't I?

"I want 1,000 carats total of grade A, 95% VVS raw gemstones, rubies, sapphires, emeralds and diamonds. The mix isn't that important but at least 100 carats of each. Donate $100,000 to the local food bank of the city where the deceased family lived. I'll send you the location where I want the gemstones sent; half within a week, the other half when I'm done."

A brief pause followed by "Agreed."

After the call was over, he made another call.

"Yes T.B., what do you think?" asked Laurent.

"Whoever he was, he wants one of the American Vampire Council killed, with their family. That could start a war.

I'm not sure if that's needed, though it is profitable. However, I don't care if it's needed, desired or would be a bad thing. The customer pays, I do my job."

"Thanks, T.B. I'll send your fee in the morning."

CHAPTER 17

Ashland, Ohio-Agate's House

Zephrin and Brielle took the map down from the wall in Agate's workshop and brought it downstairs. Zephrin had found some of his personal jerky, a culatello, but with his father's new blood meal coating. Fortunately, it was in its packing from Bulgaria.

"What is that you're eating?"

"Italian culatello, but with a Bulgarian rub, it's an acquired taste."

"Let me try some."

"Uh, okay," as he handed the package over to her.

"My dad makes the rub and added it as a coating to the culatello. I have a place in Venice that makes the culatello for me. I sent enough to Dad to make some for me and Agate. What do you think of it?"

Brielle had taken a bite and her expression was promising.

"Not bad, though it has an unexpected spicy, cinnamon flavor. There's something else, a light taste I can't place. Oh well, not bad. I'll have another."

"Good. Okay, now for the map. Do any of these pins designate locations with caves?"

Brielle studied the map for several minutes.

"There is a place not that far away. I can't remember its name. A tourist destination that gives tours. Also, what she said about the devil leaping across. Let me check." She took out her cell phone and typed.

"I thought so. Seneca Caves in Bellevue, and yes, there is a pin there and they have a place called Devil's Leap. Zephrin, why would Agate hide there?"

"I don't know, Brielle. It sounds so unlike her. Maybe that's why." That's an excellent question. There's something going on that I don't know.

"Perhaps, the web site does say that it recently closed for the year."

"How far is it?"

"An hour, however, you got a local guide. I'm not a Sherpa but I'm the next best thing, so it won't take that long."

***

Zarkhof was in his office when his business phone rang. He hit the speaker button.

"This is Zarkhof, to whom am I speaking?"

"Dr. Tashkent, this is Dr. Robin Meyers. I called to talk to you about my blood results."

"Oh yes, but please, call me Zarkhof, Dr. Meyers."

"Of course, and I'm Robin. When I got my results back, I thought a mistake had been made. I trusted who did the work, but still I had the test run a second time. The anemic victim, Jay Syne, had an extremely unusual reading."

"Dr. Meyers let me guess. He had leukemia but they were mature white blood cells, and he was blood type AB. You might find that the white blood cells have the AB antigen on them."

"But how…?"

"That's the same as my victim, Mr. Dunbar, and I don't know how. Now, did you receive a stop autopsy request from a synagogue in Montana?"

"Why yes, we did. Syne's sister claimed the body today."

"Our body was claimed by a temple representative, today. I'm not a believer is such unusual coincidences. There is a connection between them, besides their blood similarity or maybe because of it."

"Okay, say there is, doesn't mean it's illegal and we've no clue where to start."

"Do you think that exposure to radiation, could account for the AB antigen being on the white blood cells?"

"I don't know. Maybe. White blood cells are produced in the bone marrow. Radiation would destroy the marrow. Could the radiation mutate it? Possibly. I'll think on it and check with a few friends, then get back to you."

Interstate Rt. 90E

"Wake up team. We just entered Ohio and my trip adviser indicates about three hours to our destination."

"William, I've been meaning to ask, why the Toronto Spelunkers Club?" said Angela.

"I didn't want to lie, that much, to the nice man, so I bent a few things. Border guards are trained to be suspicious. I gave him something to be suspicious about. A spelunker's club is so out there, I figured he'd ask to see our equipment, which we do have. We did come from Toronto and we are going spelunking, and we do belong to a club, of sorts. A lie is a verbal statement of untruth. I never told an untruth. Granted, I obfuscated so much, we all heard the truth creak and bend under my twisting."

"Okay, Sir Galahad, we all know the truth is your Holy Grail," said Larry.

"Larry, you've always been jealous of my lineage, a direct descendant of Sir Galahad."

"He was a bastard, what's to be jealous of."

"He was, just like your grandmother, Violeta, was a courtesan. That's all irrelevant. Where we came from has no bearing on who we are. I wanted to know my lineage. You had no care about knowing yours. So, what, the friendship we have is much more important. Preserving our vampire race is next in importance. Henriette, you know her as Agate, is one of our founding members. She's chosen a path, which puts her at odds with her grandson,

Zephrin Ivano. It also seems that Laurent Fortesque, is also her grandson. Now, our job is to rescue her, before either of those two killers get to her. Killing is killing, they would both murder her out of self-preservation or a twisted form of scientific research, more akin to being sadistic than the research our lab does. Our job is to retrieve her, protect her and help her, until Dr. West finds a cure. You have the files of the known, and probable, people doing the hunting. The file labeled Fortesque bears an indication that accidents can happen, regardless of how much one is safety conscious. The file labeled Ivano, bears an indication that killing is only as a last resort. Pictures and descriptions for Zephrin and Laurent are included."

CHAPTER 18

Ashland, Ohio

"What about your classes? You are a teacher with responsibilities to your students. Wouldn't Agate want you to keep to those? Agate is in hiding and we don't know where Laurent is. You might not be safe right now but being on campus will keep Laurent from doing anything especially once I leave. He'd be most likely to follow me."

"Zephrin, I told you I'm on medical leave due to the trauma of the robbery the other night, I've posted assignments for them to do online and I'll check them. The college is okay with this as it's been done in the past, for certain circumstances. I did that for this and next week, with instructions and expectations for any work they are to do."

"Well, I'm not thrilled but at least we are together if anything happens, so welcome aboard, navigator. Our first stop will be your house, so you can get some things. Then we'll go to my hotel in Cleveland, have a nice meal, good night's sleep and check on a few things. Unfortunately, there are no Bulgarian restaurants near the hotel. However, there is a nice Italian one."

They stopped at Brielle's house, so she could collect some clothes and a few sundry items. Which turned into a large suitcase and carry-on.

"So, what's the family of an international man of mystery like?" Brielle asked.

"My parents are Sebastian and Talrya, they're geologists at the mining company Dad owns. Mom's still the scientist but Dad's the CEO type, his golf game is still worse than mine. Mom's always worried about me getting hurt, due to my job. Dad trusts me and well, they're like many CEO couples, hardworking and well off. For better or worse, I'm an only child. Mom likes the science part of her job very much. Growing up, I spent a fair amount of time with Agate, outside of Paris. I went to the University of National and World Economy, in Sofia. After that, I traveled for a year, relocating to Venice. I joined the Italian army then the Carabinieri. After my tour I became an Italian citizen and settled in to work for my company I.S.I.A. Okay, you're in the hot seat now."

"That'll be a hard bio to beat. I was born in Wilmington, Delaware. My dad, Francis, was a fire chief and my mother, Marjorie, was a para legal. They won the state lottery and retired to Bismarck, North Dakota. They died a few years later when I was seven. I've an older brother, Timothy, who I told you about. He helped me buy my house. He's the head surgeon at the Saint Alexius Medical Center, in Bismarck. My younger sister, Galadriel, yes after the elf queen, is married. They live in Cheyenne, Wyoming. She's an English teacher. My brother in law, Robert, works for Magpul Industries."

"Brielle, so how did you end up at Ashland University?"

"I've always like art. Drawing and painting and some pottery. I won several local and state art contests while in school. The first when I was six, in first grade. My drawing of the first Thanksgiving meal, won for the entire school district. I won a lot of contests and was beating college students, when I was in tenth grade. I started getting letters from recruiters about going to their colleges. Carnegie Mellon, Rhode Island School of Design, Temple, and Stanford. They all offered me a partial scholarship. Money wasn't the issue. I visited them and they were nice, but I was part of a group. Then I got a call from an old lady, Professor Agate d'Estange, of Ashland College, they hadn't changed it to University yet. She came to meet me and my family. She looked at my art and asked to watch me do some painting. She stayed for the weekend and before she left, gave me a letter of acceptance, with a full scholarship. I just so loved her personal touch and interaction. She made me feel important. She told me that every bright gemstone found is raw and needs cutting and polishing before being graded. To me, that meant the hard work that she and I would be doing. So, I spent four years there, getting my bachelors. After my graduation, Agate asked if I'd like to be her Graduate Assistant, while working on my masters. I never spent such a hard and busy year, working for and with Professor Agate."

They pulled into the hotel parking lot and took the elevator up to the 3rd floor. As they entered Zephrin's room, he said, "There's fresh fruit on the counter and San Pellegrino in the fridge. I'm taking a shower. You can take one after, if you want. If you didn't bring any or enough clothes, call the front desk, tell them what you want and in what size and it'll be delivered."

"But Zephrin, that'll cost."

"True, but my weekly allowance will cover it; besides, remember what I told you the other day?"

"Oh, that's right, you own the company. Just how rich are you?"

"I don't know or care. Now, if you know of any places that make collectible glass that would be a place I'd like to visit."

Zephrin went to take his shower, while Brielle tried some of the San Pellegrino, which tasted like a mimosa but not as sweet. She took a banana and saw Zephrin's laptop, on the table. Its screen saver was on, pictures of World War Two airplanes and a song was playing, the Tarantella. She noticed a wireless microphone next to the computer.

"One of those remote microphones. Let me see, Siri, please play the songs Big Spender and Goldfinger by Shirley Bassey."

"My name is not Siri, I'm Gina and who are you?" came a voice, from the computer.

"Oh, I see, Zephrin gave the program a new name."

"Well…no. Gina gave Zephrin's computer people the information to write the program about Gina. Gina's parents named her Gina. However, let's get back to Gina's question, who are you?"

"My name is Brielle Chalmers. Now, could you play the songs I asked for?"

"Those are excellent songs by my good friend." The songs Brielle requested started playing.

As the song Goldfinger ended, Zephrin came into the room. Hair a bit damp but with a cologne that smelled rather good.

"Who or what is Gina?"

"Oh, I see you've met her. Gina is a computer personal assistant, sort of like Siri on steroids."

"Zephrin, Gina resents that. Gina has never used steroids. The closest Gina's ever come to a steroid is Hi-Fi stereo. Zephrin, pay attention to the next song," as Big Spender began playing.

"Gina's a computer program?"

"Brielle, dear, please. Excel is a computer program. Adobe is a computer program. Please don't insult Gina, as Gina hasn't insulted you."

"Gina's not a program. She's the A.I. of my main frame back in Italy. Gina is tied into my laptop and is connected to my home in Venice."

"That's right, you're Italian. You have no accent at all. Besides, I initially figured you were French, as Agate came from Paris. So, Gina is a prototype?"

"No, when I came up with the idea, I contacted many experts in computer A.I functions. Agate mentioned a few she knew in France and Poland. They provide a basic formatting program for my people to work with."

***

On the fourth floor, Laurent was listening to the conversation.

"Mon ami, just why did you bring the art teacher with you? She's okay but, to each their own. Speaking of own, I didn't know until now that you owned ISIA. That makes you extraordinarily rich and even more dangerous if you ever learn how to use that wealth. I thought everything was from mom and dad."

Gina announced. "Zephrin, a call from your father just came into your cell phone."

"Thanks, Gina. Brielle, if you'll excuse me for a bit, I'll go take my dad's call." as he went into the bedroom.

***

On the floor above, Laurent was listening to the bugs he had planted. "Se la vie, there are drawbacks to the bedroom being private. Yet, I'm sure daddy is letting the cat out of the bag, so to speak."

***

"Yes Dad, what's up?"

"Your mother told me what's up and you should know that Laurent is also looking and what's even more of a concern. A trusted source told me that the A.V.C has issued a no on two requests. One for war and another was a request for your death. I've already spoken to Alu'Card, the head of

~ 175 ~

our Council of Princes. He said he'd ask the American's who, what and why."

"You mean that someone in America wants a war! The last one got a lot of us and humans killed. It solved nothing. Oh, I know about Laurent, so that answers the request about me."

"How did you find out?"

"Simple, I went to college."

"What do you mean?"

"I was following up on Mom asking me to check in to Agate going missing. Laurent was at the same college and saw me."

"Yes, and I find it very coincidental that this request was made after you had arrived in America. I want you home now, son."

"Dad, I know where Agate is, and I need to find her just so Laurent and his gang of sociopathic torturers don't. If they don't have permission, they won't kill me because that would start a war."

"Okay, son, I know that Agate would want it to be you. Please, take care, I love you. Remember, they may not care about the denial."

"Love you both, bye."

Zephrin, emerged from the bedroom, a concerned look on his face.

"So, how's your dad doing, Zephrin?" Brielle asked.

"Oh, he's fine, thanks for asking. He just had some family business to talk about. There's a lot of concern about Agate. However, I did promise you a dinner. There's a nice Italian place about two blocks away called That's a Spicy Meatball."

"Sure, Italian sounds great." She replied with a wink.

They walked to the restaurant. A nice quaint setting, no booths. Only tables with candles, homemade tablecloths, and shakers, one of garlic with cheese and one with crushed peppers. There was cruet of olive oil.

A short, plump Italian lady greeted them.

"Oh, look at you, what a lovely couple. Welcome to our kitchen for families, please follow me. Would you like a drink while you decide on your meal?"

"Yes, please a Negroni for me and a Campari and soda for my companion."

As the lady left, Zephrin said, "You don't mind me ordering for you?"

"Go ahead, I'm interested in seeing what you think I'd like. Don't worry, I promise to eat whatever you order."

She returned with the drinks. "Would you like a menu?"

"That won't be needed. We'll start with bruschetta pizzaiola, then a pasta al'Forno, for the main dish, meatballs in white wine sauce. For dessert, some gelato affogato."

"Very excellent choices, signore, thank you."

The meal began as the bruschetta arrived and as they finished, a man walked up to their table, it was Laurent.

"Mon ami, Zephrin Ivano, so unexpected to see you here and in such beautiful company. It looks like pleasure, yet you are a long way from home, so perhaps it's business as well, eh?" Laurent said in French.

Zephrin looked up as his hand moved over his knife. "I could well say the same thing, Laurent, but I don't see any wild boars nearby."

"Oh my, such a sense of humor and on that subject, how's your grandmother doing? Ah, to be in the twilight of her years, the sun beginning to set on such a wonderful life. I hope I'm there to pay my respects when she does pass. Her art and pottery are extraordinary. Well, enough of the pleasantries. Enjoy your meal and evening. I always get what I want, even if it means that a teaching position would become open at that college."

"She's not involved, Laurent. What is it Americans say…You want a shot at the title?"

"In time, mon ami, in due time. However, I didn't mean your guest. Now, I'll go pay for your meal, so eat up and enjoy."

Brielle, without taking her eyes from her plate said. "Tsigane."

For one of the very few times in his life, Laurent was shocked, almost stunned. Not only at what he was called but the realization that Brielle had understood everything that was said.

"Touché, Brielle Chalmers, I hope to return the favor in the future."

Laurent went to the register and spoke to the lady who had served them. He handed her some money and left.

"I'm sorry about that, Brielle. He ruined the meal and evening."

"No, he didn't, Zephrin. The food still tastes great and it would be rude to leave before finishing. As for the evening being ruined, that is still in the future. That's the man Agate wants you to protect me from?"

"Yes, he's the head of Al-Jazeera in America and has a beef with me."

On their way back to his hotel room, Zephrin asked,

"Brielle, how did you know he was a gypsy? Laurent is a very educated and deceptive sociopath. A murdering piece of shit, if you'll excuse my language but he doesn't look like a typical gypsy."

"Yes, his accent is much more southern French but it's rhythm and bounce are that of a gypsy. He might have been adopted by them when he was young. I see why you were concerned about me and why Agate is hiding from him. Anyone who would approach you in public and make such threats, I mean, even paying for our meal. Besides, Agate never said anything about Laurent, but she did hate gypsies."

As they went inside Zephrin's hotel room, he asked,

"Gina, any calls while we were at dinner?"

"No, Zephrin."

He started pacing the room, muttering in Italian. Brielle walked up to him and placed her arms around his neck and kissed him. She pulled back and looked at him.

"That was nice but what's wrong? Oh, I shouldn't have done that?"

"Not at all, I'm just very distracted. It was nice, genuinely nice, as a matter of fact. It has to do with what I haven't or can't tell you and no, I'm not married, and neither is there a current significant other."

Gina chimed in. "That's correct, Ms. Chalmers. Zephy hasn't had a significant other in well, several years."

"Zephy?" Brielle said as a smile came to her face. She placed a hand over her mouth to hide it.

"Yes, my mother and Agate would call me that and somehow it was placed into Gina's programming."

"Okay, Zephy. I'm curious as to how Laurent knew where we were eating dinner. I mean he'd have to have been watching the hotel for a long time to be able to follow us."

His eyes narrowed at her question. He looked around the room, his gaze stopping at the door to the balcony as he just shook his head. He then took Brielle's hand and led her onto the balcony, closing the door.

"Well though a bit chilly, it is romantic," as she kissed him again.

"Laurent must have gotten into my room and planted some bugs. Wait here, I'll be back shortly," He said as he took his jacket off and placed it over Brielle's shoulders.

Zephrin went to the bedroom and pulled out a case. He put the shoulder holsters on and then placed the two matched pistols in them and returned to the main room.

"Gina, run security program Delta, Zeta, nine, four."

"Executing now," as a metal antenna emerged from his laptop. Five minutes later, Gina replied.

"Four devices located and neutralized."

"Thanks Gina."

"Gina's glad that she was able to help."

Zephrin went to the balcony door and opened it. Brielle looked at the guns he now wore.

"Well, it's a fashion statement to be sure, but do you really need those? I saw you take down those thugs."

"It's safe now, come back in. There were four bugs in the room. They're no longer a concern. As for the guns, the closer an enemy is, the less you should rely on guns. Laurent is just as deadly as I am in martial arts. He wouldn't give a gun a passing thought, except by me. Any thugs he hired would give them a concern."

In a room on the fourth floor, Laurent heard a screeching in his earpiece and quickly removed it.

CHAPTER 19

Bellevue, Ohio

Jania had been at the restaurant for a little over two hours, when two men came in and sat down with her.

"Hello, Jania, sorry we're late."

"Greetings, guys, long time no see. Max and Ivan Silas don't worry about being late. Tell me what you've been doing before we go to the hospital. Oh, if you're hungry, the trash potatoes are quite good. Did you get what I asked for?"

"Yes, maps and pictures of the caves. They were what we expected, most areas you're not able to stand up. The public areas you can stand but try not to jump too high and some you must bend over a bit. There are a lot of crawl spaces to check out," said Max.

"As for what we've been up to, same old same old. Families are doing well. My youngest is running for his state senate this fall," replied Ivan.

"With the way you, and most of our group feels about government? However, I do see the advantage. Being inside the establishment does allow certain advantages when the war starts. It all comes down to planning," said Jania.

"So, when do we go?"

"Relax, we've a while. I'm waiting for the sun to go down. I know, stereotypical, but that is the best time. I want us to go check the place out first before sundown. Now, I need to call Laurent, to let him know what I've found and our plans. He might be able to join us."

***

"Zephrin, maybe Laurent is the 'gypsy' referred to in Agate's painting?"

"That's some nice inductive reasoning; I'm the Cardinal with crossed swords, a warrior ready to fight and the gypsy, holding the chalice, refers to my opponent or challenge. There's a sensible logic with that thought. I wonder if there's a link between that and those words we found in the frame.

"Gina, search for the following names in art works or religious books. Watchers, Parables, Astronomy and Dreams."

"Searching, Zephy," Gina said. "Gina has the results. The only reference that contains all four words is The Book of Enoch."

"I've never heard of that book, Gina. Please describe it."

"Enoch is Noah's great grandfather and the seventh son of Adam. It's composed of four books; whose names match the four words you gave me. There is a fifth book, the Epistle. The Book of Enoch is only accepted as cannon by the Ethiopian and Eritrean Orthodox churches. It's wholly in the Ge'ez language with some fragments in Aramaic,

Greek and Latin. The first part of the Book of Enoch describes the fall of the Watchers, the angels who fathered the Nephilim. The remainder of the book describes Enoch's visits to heaven. The travels, visions and dreams, and his revelations."

"That's nice, Gina, but what the hell does it mean?" said Zephrin.

"Zephrin, the Nephilim are the offspring of the sons of God and the daughters of men."

"Did they actually exist?"

"Maybe, the giant, Goliath, is that just a parable or is it fact?"

West of Bellevue, Ohio

"Okay ladies and gents. The sun set about forty-five minutes ago, so last stop, everybody off, we thank you for driving with us. Please make sure you remove all baggage. The owners aren't responsible for any lost items," Garibaldi announced.

"Ah conductor, this isn't where we are supposed to be," said Larry.

"Give the gentleman a cigar. Yes, we're about one and a half kilometers from there. We're walking now so it's night suits, hand signals and brief communications. Don't want to drive right up in case any of those looking for Agate happen to be in the area."

They opened the trunk then equipped themselves with black night suits, visors, radio headsets and hoods. They also took a close in weapon, an eighteen-inch baton with sharp flanges at the last few inches and a modified semi-automatic pistol that can fire a special dart or regular bullet.

"Sounds good, Gari," said Angela. "East is that way." She pointed as she looked at her GPS compass.

"We're heading east, fellow spelunkers," Larry said, his smile, hidden by his hood and equipment.

The Traditionalists

Jania, Max and Ivan arrived at Seneca Caves, about thirty minutes after sunset. They parked the car about two blocks from the entrance and easily jumped the eight-foot-tall fence, about a hundred feet from the visitors building.

"Max, make sure any video equipment and security people are neutralized. A robber surprised while looking for stuff to steal. Oh, and any tapes of the security system."

"Sure thing." Max headed toward the main building.

"Okay, Ivan, we're heading for the caves. We're looking for Agate, and then we come back out. Laurent hasn't gotten back to me so he may or may not be coming. Zephrin Ivano is involved. I've no information as to his knowledge that Agate might be here. So, be aware that Zephrin might be here. If he is here or does show, well, accidents happen."

Max reached the Visitors Center. There were three fixed cameras. Two angled toward the parking lot and the third toward the cave's entrance. A signpost with an arrow, pointed the same direction. He looked in a window and saw a security guard sitting, his legs resting on the counter. There were three computer screens, one was showing a Star Wars movie, while the two others showed the parking lot and entrance leading to the visitor center, the second of the front entrance gates. Max backed up a little and jumped through the window, sending glass flying and the guard sprawling to the floor. As the guard was swearing and trying to get up, Max kicked him in the stomach, and then punched him in the side of his head. A loud crack came as the head spun around.

As the guard thudded to the ground, Max picked up the chair and slammed that into his back, with a crunching sound. Max took the man's wallet and watch, then went to the computer keyboard and began searching. The systems firewalls and passwords provided only brief resistance. He found what he was looking for. The credit card information of the visitors, with their names, for the past six months. Sure enough, Agate D'Estange was in the records. He pulled out a flash drive and downloaded that information, then erased it. He deleted the security recordings and erased the tape backups. Then he opened all the cabinets and drawers. He tossed the contents on the floor and turned the lights off. "Mom always said to save electricity."

The Rescuers

Ten minutes after they left their car, the stealthily clad Garibaldi, Angela, and Larry reached a side fence for the Seneca Caves, jumped the fence with ease, and landing about ten feet beyond. They checked the monitors on their wrists. A red dot now faintly showed.

Angela said, "Target in range about four hundred feet away and eighty feet below us."

"Okay, Angela has point, Larry to her left; I'm on the right. We'll go in through the exit. Hand signals from here out, don't know if the caves will affect the radio, so don't rely on them," said Garibaldi.

The Traditionalists

Laurent arrived at the Seneca Caves about an hour after leaving the hotel. Checking his watch, If Zephrin is coming I've got an hour before he arrives. He called Jania.

"Yes, Laurent, not the best reception. Ivan and Max Silas are with me, in what's called the Foyer and we'll wait for you. Go down the path and then down the steps, we'll be there. Security has been neutralized."

"Great, be there in a bit."

When Laurent arrived, Jania and the Silas brothers, were in the Foyer. A roughly thirty-foot-long by twenty-foot-wide cavern that might have been six or seven feet high. Max and Ivan, were looking at a map, using their cell phones for light.

"Well, well, well, if it isn't the three blind mice."

"This place is huge, and we can't just turn on the lights," Ivan sneered.

"Jania, I know where not to look."

Max said. "Okay, where don't we look, bright eyes?"

"Simple, Jania, you look in the most out of the way place here, someplace where the tourists don't go. She's hiding. Despite bad jokes you can hide something or someone in plain sight because people don't know how, where, or even to look. She's waiting for Zephrin to find her and he'll be coming. We've got about an hour. He neutralized my bugs, so I can only venture a guess. He knows I'm here and looking, so I'd bet on his arrival."

The three looked at him and Jania grabbed the map from Ivan.

"Okay, there's this Devil's Leap, which leads to a Wild Caves section, where that boy died when he fell…or did he fall? We've got two options, head all the way down to this underground river and swim over or go down Devil's Leap and climb."

Laurent just shook his head. "If that human boy found her, then she killed him, and the police came and checked the area out. Oh, Agate was there but she moved to a different location, we need to figure out where. A place fairly easy to reach and yet, especially now, that people wouldn't go to."

The Rescuers

At the exit to the caves, Garibaldi, Angela, and Larry stopped. Garibaldi pointed to his GPS monitor and pressed a button, which sent a response signal to Agate's signal. On all their monitors, the red dot, now showed them seventy feet above and forty feet away from their target. Garibaldi gave the signal to head into the caves.

The Couple

Zephrin and Brielle pulled into the almost empty parking lot, past the sign that said closed for the season. There was one car in the lot, near the gate.

"Well I don't see any security, but I'm sure they have cameras. One car parked here, probably the security guards."

"Why? What is there to steal at a place like this, Zephrin?"

"More than you might think but it's more to protect themselves from people entering the caves without permission and supervision. If someone did and got hurt, then there would be a lawsuit."

They approached the entrance and jumped the turnstile. Zephrin saw the cameras, they weren't moving, and all the outdoor lights were off. Someone turned the security system off. They headed for the main building when he stepped on some broken glass. Zephrin smelled it…fresh blood, as he looked in. There had been a fight, he saw a body lying on the floor, face down, a broken chair on top of it.

"Brielle, someone got here before us. This won't be a safe place for you."

"Who, Laurent?" She started smelling the air and she made a scrunching face. "That's a bad smell."

"Yes, excrement as the muscles let go when a person dies."

"I was afraid of that."

"So, where do I look for Agate?"

"Zephrin, there should be a stand inside the door with maps, get one."

He kicked the window in and opened the dead bolt with his handkerchief covered hand. He returned with the maps.

"Okay, let's go."

"Not so fast, little rabbit. I doubt it was Laurent. Granted, he's a killer, but with finesse, not brute force. That in there was plainly a sadistic killing. It was friends of his. They may well know that I'll be or could be coming. Next, I don't know where to look. This is a big place; he's probably got help and will plan on my arrival."

"So, he won't be expecting me?" Brielle stated with an air of defiance.

"Brielle, these won't be unexpected thugs. They'll be killers, close to me with martial arts."

"So, you think my waiting in the car will be safer? If something happens to you, I'd be unaware and like a bird in a cage, as the cats come to get me."

This is a bad idea, but so is leaving her behind. "Okay, it's slightly better for you to be with me, than alone."

The Traditionalists

The sound of a clattering stone echoed in the caves.

Laurent, Jania, Max and Ivan, stopped as they heard the echoing stone bouncing.

"That wasn't from where we came," said Ivan, it was in the other direction. Looking at the map, he smiled. "Smart, this Zephrin came in using the exit."

"I told you Zephrin would be here, a bit early but still not unexpected," said Laurent. "Let's go have some fun." The four of them headed off toward the caverns exit. The noise they made, despite their amateur attempts at being quiet, was heard by Agate's rescuers. They stopped. Angela, being on the walkway, went prone, her auto pistol out. She saw three bodies coming toward them and aimed at the closest and fired, a pfft sound was all it made.

Max yelled. "I've been shot, son of a bitch! I'll rip Zephrin's head off for that."

Max had been shot before, along with stabbed, sliced and crunched. This was more like the pain of shrapnel. It was a hot biting pain.

He reached for the wound and felt something sticking it him. "Shit, a dart. Zephrin shot me with a dart gun."

He pulled the dart out, about half the size of his thumb.

"You okay?" yelled Jania

"Yeah, it's only a flesh wound but I'm feeling a bit dizzy and nauseous."

Laurent knew. That's not Zephrin. He'd use a real gun, of which he has two particularly good ones. Laurent focused on the area ahead. The darkness faded. He saw three figures, one on the walkway, prone and one to either side, crouching behind the point figure. Laurent measured the distance and height of the ceiling. I can make it.

"Jania, get Max out of here, he's been poisoned. Ivan, take the one on the right of the walkway."

He jumped toward the prone figure on the walkway. They dropped the pistol and sprang up, only to have Laurent's foot, slam into their chest. Angela was sent crashing into the stone wall. Her head just missing a rock outcrop. Jania went to Max and helped support him as they walked back to the Foyer. They reached the foyer about the same time Zephrin and Brielle did.

Zephrin and Brielle headed into the caves. They reached the bottom of the stairs when they heard a female voice.

"It's okay, Max, I'll get you out of here."

"God my shoulder hurts, Jania. Thanks for helping me, that bastard Zephrin will get his, I swear it!"

"Why Max Silas and Jania Mikos, don't you know swearing isn't something to do lightly, you never know who's listening," Zephrin said as he smiled.

"Oh my, what do we have here? Why it's a wayward prince and his mistress."

"Jania Mikos, amazing what the saber tooth tiger does drag in. That was probably Max's handiwork back there, not that you aren't capable, but not you're style."

Jania noticed the look on Brielle's face, shock, surprise, horror, and longing, all rolled into one.

"Oh, dear, you're not his mistress, or are you? Zephrin is a love and leave kind of guy, I don't know who you are, but you'd better run a long home. Zephrin's quest for his Baba, ends here. It's a duel, Zephy, you and me. She can watch, but then I'd have to kill her after she watched me kill you. If she left now, got into her car, and just drove, it might be hard to find her."

"Jania, you've no idea what you've just asked for."

"Oh, I've got a clue, because even if I do lose, I've opened up a new chapter in your relationship. Something let your mind make an awfully bad decision, Zephrin."

"Somehow, Jania, I don't think you're considering 'first blood' as the winner."

***

In a small tunnel off the 'West Hall,' Agate felt a soft vibration on her chest. Agate stirred to life. "Thank God they're here. Now, to go greet my rescuers."

Rescuers and Traditionalists

"Laurent is mine, Larry, you handle Ivan, we'll check on Angela later."

As Laurent and Ivan fought Garibaldi and Larry. It became quickly clear that all were vampires. Humans didn't learn Draco Vydra.

"We're not here to hurt anyone, Laurent. We are here for Agate, to keep her from you and Zephrin."

"You are much too late for that. I've been looking for her for a long, long time, and no little piece of shit like you, with your disrespect of our traditions, will stop me. How dare you shoot a vampire with a gun and not engage in hand-to-hand or a duel."

"Traditions evolve, change. They fade out of style, only to be replaced. I never thought that torture was a tradition. It's a psychopathic oddity of people with small minds."

Laurent jumped the ten feet or so and landed close enough to lash at the ninja garbed figure, with a kick.

"Didn't anyone tell you that vampire ninjas went out of style last decade?" Laurent taunted.

"I'll make a note of telling Abercrombie and Fitch," was Garibaldi's reply.

"We seek to ensure our survival. We are the apex hunter. You vampires who think of blending in with the humans are pathetic. Zephrin will be here soon, so how his help beat him here, I don't know, but you can all die together."

"We're not with Zephrin, Laurent. So, this just might be like the end of that spaghetti western…The Good, The Bad and you."

Laurent was impressed with his opponents Draco Vydra skill, not as good as his, but still particularly good. His companion was as well, a little better than Ivan was, as Ivan was slowly backing up. This forced Laurent to give ground, to avoid being flanked.

Jania and Zephrin

Jania put Max on the floor, his back against the wall, then Zephrin and Jania moved to about fifteen feet from each other. She bowed, in the traditional manner, before a Draco Vydra duel, arms crossed, then open as you bow, empty palms to your opponent.

"Oh, how quaint, she's going to stay and watch. You should get some popcorn and a drink, you're an honored guest, the first human in an awfully long time that's seen a vampire Draco Vydra duel. The only weapons used are what are in the ring, so to speak."

Brielle looked at the two of them…Human? Vampire?

"I can tell that you're confused, that's okay. As I said, dear, Zephrin will have a lot of explaining to do, in the unlikely event he wins. I'll have no problem explaining after I win."

"Jania, a big mouth goes with a big ego. It also depends on what you think needs explaining. You're just helping the brother of a convicted terrorist with his revenge."

She's right, once I've disposed of Jania, I'll have a much harder time explaining this away. Brielle will have my head for lying to her, again.

They bowed. Zephrin took a traditional defensive position, crossed swords. Jania took up the viper attack position. She cartwheeled toward Zephrin, who backed up. When she stopped, Zephrin charged. Jania blocked his blows and countered with a leg sweep, to which Zephrin jumped, just to feel a fist strike his leg. He kicked with the other leg and landed on her shoulder.

As Brielle watched, several of the moves looked like what her brother had taught her. The duel continued for at least five minutes. Each was landing and blocking blows. Zephrin had a bad cut on his cheek from a rock that Jania had used. She had a bloody nose. They both were limping. Brielle saw a single figure was moving up the stairway, behind the fight. She also saw four others, who were using martial arts, come from the opposite side of the cavern.

Laurent was keeping Garibaldi at bay but gaining more respect for his Vydra skill as he was backing up to the foyer. Ivan was giving it his all but was clearly losing. Both

Laurent and Ivan were bleeding from several cuts and their ninja dressed opponents, had matching blood stains on their clothes.

Brielle recognized the single figure and she screamed Agate's name.

Agate reached the foyer, she saw Zephrin and another fighting with Draco Vydra with a third watching…It was Brielle! The she heard Brielle scream her name.

The smell of blood was strong, and the urge was growing, and she was almost powerless to hold it back.

Jania landed a blow to Zephrin's gut. He doubled over and she went to knee him in the face but only landed on the side of his head. He tucked and rolled past her, landing on his knees. He reached up and behind, grabbing a solid handful of Jamia's hair and pulling down. The back of her head slammed into the ground and he rolled over punching her in the face with a rock he'd picked up. Her face exploded with blood as she sprawled to the ground.

Agate then heard familiar voices…Laurent's and Colonel Garibaldi's, as the craving took control.

"NOOOOOO!"

The power of her voice was such that everyone stopped and turned. They all recognized who had yelled. Yet her appearance was not that of the grandmother next door. It was a caricature of such. She was taller, her muscles noticeably larger and she had fangs.

"So, you want duels! I will teach you all about what duels really look like! You both thought that you could handle me. Ignorant fools!"

She sprang toward Laurent. Flailing at him with her hands. Laurent reeled under her powerful blows, realizing too late the blows had a second purpose. Agate grabbed his shirt and flung him into a cave wall. She wheeled and then ran toward Zephrin. He tried to jump away, but not before taking a forearm slam that knocked him back, tumbling about ten feet.

"Leave, Brielle, and forget everything you saw or heard here. Zephrin, Laurent and I, all have sins to atone for." Agate turned to look at both Laurent and Zephrin.

"Laurent, you think you can control me! You think that this can be harnessed," as she gestured to herself, arms wide open. "Laurent Fortesque, I am hatred for life! I am pure lustful desire. I am evil. You both forgot the stories we created to scare the humans weren't just stories; this can't be controlled or contained. You, Zephrin you're just as pathetic as my other grandson. You think that killing me is the humane course, like I'm a sick animal. It's for the survival of all vampires; the needs of the many outweigh the needs of the few, right Prince Zephy? Yet, did you ever try to see our needs? No, you removed us like an infected dog."

Laurent coughed as he slowly got to his feet. While everyone was listening to Agate, Colonel Garibaldi was aiming his pistol at Agate, holding it with both hands. I'll have one chance. He waited...come on, guys move out of my line of sight! They shifted as Laurent spoke to Zephrin and Agate moved forward...

"You called Zephrin your other grandson you don't have two grandsons…unless."

"Mon ami, isn't that what you say Prince Laurent? You and Zephrin are half-brothers and that is my sin. You both think you're smart, I'd say you could figure it out, if I let you both live but, ce la vie."

Three pft's were heard and Agate screamed as three darts lodged in her and she slowly dropped to her knees and then lay on the ground. Colonel Garibaldi stepped toward Agate, with Larry close behind him, and spoke to the group.

"My name is Lt. Colonel William Garibaldi and we are from…a group that Agate helped start. Please allow us to take her so that no more here will die. She'll be very well cared for, I promise. Then if you two want to continue fighting, go ahead."

Laurent coughed up some blood and his breathing hurt like hell. He figured he had a punctured lung and a few broken ribs. Zephrin and Jania didn't look much better. What seemed like a half hour passed before one of them spoke.

"Well, mon ami?" as he looked at Zephrin.

"Why should I trust you, Colonel?"

"There's little I can tell you. But it was Agate who asked us to help you with Gina."

"Okay Colonel, go ahead, you'll do more for Agate than either one of us would have done," said Zephrin.

"I'm afraid I don't agree, Colonel. I've many questions. The first of which is how they hell can we be half-brothers?" Laurent replied.

"Laurent, I can't tell you what I don't know. I do know that I've got to get Agate to a safe place where she can get help, so I'm afraid this family reunion must come to an end. I'll ask Agate to call either of you or both when she wakes up." Garibaldi and Larry left, carrying Agate.

"Well then, that kind of changes things doesn't it, Zephy? Not every day you find out that the person you're trying to kill, might be your long-lost half-brother. However, in the interest of brotherly love and knowing what God did to Cain, why don't we all just go our separate ways? Oh, we'll clean the place up. Besides, I want to kill you when we're both in good shape, so consider this a reprieve until sometime in the future."

"Sounds okay with me, Laurent, we'll be going."

As they got into the car, Brielle said. "I'll take my time driving home, is an hour drive home enough time?"

"I doubt it."

CHAPTER 20

A Plane over Colorado

The plane went into auto pilot at 31,000 feet. The floor hatch to the luggage compartment opened and Taraz Bulba, wearing a gas mask, emerged. He was also wearing a sky diving suit. He checked the passengers; all were out cold, including the pilot and co-pilot. He went over to the door. It's been a long time since I've done this. Parachuting from a plane into a heavy forest. The only difference is, this time there is no suitcase full of money, to get tangled up in the trees. So, it's Pikes Peak instead of Mt. Saint Helens but no witnesses this time.

He opened the door and was immediately sucked out of the plane, followed by most everything not tied down. He landed in a wooded area, collected his parachute, took out his cell phone and checked the GPS. Good, not that far off.

He called a number, "Dr. Daniels, check the morning news. I'll expect payment within the week."

"Thanks, Taraz."

"If you say so, just remember be careful about what you wish for."   Dr. Daniels called another number.

Laurent's phone vibrated; he saw it was Daniels.

"Laurent here, how may I be of service?"

"As of now, the American Vampire Council is unable to punish you for killing Zephrin."

"Well isn't that a case of bad timing. Not that I really care, but still bad timing. Unfortunately, it's become a bit complicated. My question is, why do you think that being punished would be of any concern of mine?"

"You've always hated Zephrin and he'd be in the way of capturing Agate, so I just made it easier for you to do both."

"Why and how?" asked Javier.

"It was your suggestion that led me down that path. Those that chose the time for action, control said action, especially when it's war."

Cleveland, Ohio

After arriving back at Zephrin's hotel room, he motioned for Brielle to be quiet. He went to the bedroom and came back with his laptop.

"Gina, are you there?"

The small antenna emerged from the computer. Followed by an image of an extremely attractive lady in a demure, red, and green, full length dress appeared on the wall.

"Zephrin, Gina is always here at your beck and call. Oh, you have company. Hello, Brielle, a pleasure to see you. Zephy, what the hell happened to you?"

"Hello, Gina. We had an unexpected run-in with Laurent."

"Gina, has there been word from Mom or Dad, while we were gone?"

"No."

"Okay, Gina search about anything associated with Laurent Fortesque's history. Compare that to my mom's and Agate's history before she married my dad, the first time."

Gina's image vanished from the wall.

"Okay, can you give me a synopsis of what I just saw? Then I'll decide if I'll take your head off."

"Agate, like me, is a vampire, she's around four hundred years old. Some old vampires become trapped with blood lust, maybe dementia, which is Latin for demon-madness."

"Very good, Zephy, you paid attention to your history lessons."

"You mean that vampires exist?"

"Yes."

"But how can that be?"

"The technology for Gina isn't awfully hard to do. From your cell phone now, people video chat, they can make videos, and play games. Siri can do searches; remind you of important dates, events, and other things at a command. Gina is just a bigger, more advanced version. By the same extension, vampires are only human, we're just a mutation.

"Okay Zephrin, let's start with the explanation. What did I see back there?"

"You saw a good friend and mentor, showing the signs of a mental affliction-dementia. I saw my grandmother's mind give into a craving, like a junkie does."

"What I saw was a sixty-five-year-old lady, toss two adult men at least ten feet in the air with minimal effort. I heard this same lady and Jania, call you all vampires, who don't exist except in games and books; yet Agate looked very much like such a creature. I saw you and Jania fighting to the death, in a ritual duel, that she said humans haven't seen in an awfully long time."

"Okay, I'll start with the vampire part. Why couldn't vampires exist?"

"Vampires are based on Prince Vlad Dracula, known as Vlad the Impaler, as told by Bram Stoker."

"Your point being?"

"Vampires would've been revealed by now. They need human blood to survive. That 'craving' as you put it couldn't be hidden, especially with modern technology. Agate can't be a vampire and you can't be a vampire. Vampires don't exist and yes, I'm trying to rationalize that what I saw isn't pure fantasy."

"We vampires created such an image to help better hide our existence. Bram Stoker had a friend, Armin Vambery, who was a vampire. He, though never telling Bram that, did tell Bram about a relative and how he had died, due to a mental disease. Bram, damn him to hell, took that information and wrote his book. Armin was the nephew of Vlad Tepes and Agate is Armin's sister. Armin's niece, Talrya Nekos, is my mother. That makes Count Dracula, Vlad Draculea, my Great, Great Uncle."

"You're serious! You believe what you just said. If what you say it true, why did she have fangs and you don't? Are they retractable, like claws?'

"Fangs are the body's reaction to the uncontrollable craving for blood. They aren't retractable but develop very quickly from our incisors. Simply put, I don't have fangs because I don't need them."

"That's right; fangs are to suck the blood out of a person's neck."

"Fangs aren't straws; they're more like neck openers. The human mouth was not designed to do that. Once the skin has been torn open, the blood can be lapped up or we could sip it like being at a drinking fountain. However, we don't need human blood, any blood will do, except for vampire blood. That makes us sick, though in a pinch it was done back in the olden days. However, if you're suffering from the sickness, vampire blood has no ill-effects on you. If you would note, in many cultures, blood is an ingredient in cooking, cow, pigs, and chickens' blood mainly."

At that, Brielle, grabbed the dish of fruit and sent it sailing at him, he ducked, though an apple did bounce off his head as she ran into the bathroom, locking the door.

"I should call the police and tell them what happened."

"If you want to, go ahead, I won't stop you. I'll even slide the phone from your purse under the door for you to use. But think what their reaction would be when you tell them."

"Yeah, maybe, I don't know. Vampires can't abide sunlight and are repelled by a cross. You're out in broad daylight without any problems."

"Sunlight only affects those with the mental break down. Otherwise, we just need to use a good sunscreen when at the beach. The aversion to silver crosses is a function of history and technology. Back in the day, many crosses were made of silver and a rather poor process, led to a noticeable amount of silver nitrate, which we call 'luna caustic.' Silver nitrate would be mixed with holy water and was used for antiseptic properties. Well, we vampires are allergic to this. It doesn't kill, except in massive doses but it causes us pain and nausea. Would you please come out of the bathroom? I'll answer all your questions and stay on the other side of the room, if it will make you feel better. If you want to leave, I'll have a cab called to take you home."

Zephrin waited about thirty seconds before he heard the door unlock. Brielle came out, her mascara running down her checks from the tears that had come from her red eyes. He handed her his kerchief.

"So, vampires need to eat blood at every meal?"

"Not anymore. We've developed or maybe refined is a better word, the process of using blood in common foods. Yes, we still need regular food, just like you. Transfusions have been a great help with the craving. Some pills are being tested and well, my father made a blood meal that I have used as a rub or coating for culatello."

Brielle looked at Zephrin…her eyes widened as she remembered.

"You mean that I ate vampire food? You let me eat blood! Why you asshole. Why didn't you tell me? Will I die?"

"No, you won't die. What should I've said, hey, Brielle, you don't want to eat that, it's my specially made vampire jerky? It won't hurt you in any way, I promise, and you did seem to like it."

Brielle was scrunching her face as she made gagging sounds with her mouth. She rushed to the toilet to throw up. After emptying her stomach and cleaning her face, she spoke.

"Okay, how is Laurent your half-brother? Why wouldn't your mother tell you about him?"

"That's a good question and I'll be sure to ask her about that, because I'm an only child, at least as far as I know."

"Next, why are you and Laurent enemies?"

"Vampires have two factions. Mine is Modernists and Laurent's is Traditionalists. Mine feels that blending into human society is the best path for our continued existence. If our existence ever becomes known, we'll face extinction. Laurent's side agrees with that, but they feel that we need to become humanities masters. Then treat you like cattle.

They also want all vampires to be like Agate was. They capture Sundowners afflicted vampires and do research on them. My side calls it torture. They've done this on humans in the past, all in the name of perfecting the race. They see vampires as the next step in human evolution. We both look for any Sundowners vampires, mine to put them out of their misery and Laurent's to capture for scientific research."

"So, your purpose here was to kill Agate, your grandmother, if you saw that she had this Fangs thing?"

"Yes, so, in answer to your earlier question, I am a monster."

"Who were those vampires, who took Agate?"

"I don't know, a new faction, obviously. I've never heard of a group of vampires that's out to help those affected. This will all be remarkably interesting news for my parents."

"How old are you and can you prove it?"

"I'm 117 years old and nothing I have on me can prove that. My passport has me at thirty-five. You could use your cell phone and look up the I.S.I.A. Remember that I told you I own the company? Check to see how big it is and how much it's worth. Could one person have done such in their lifetime?"

"Steve Jobs created Apple Computers in his lifetime."

"Okay, point taken, I guess that isn't proof. However, being a founder of a cutting-edge computer company is noticeably different than that of an international detective agency."

"You said you bought it ten years ago. Oh, that was another lie. Okay, what you've said is logical and possibly believable, but also almost impossible to disprove. It's okay, what creates the dependency for blood? What or why are you a vampire?"

"I did buy ISIA ten years ago. Vampirism is a mutated form of anemia, we have the same high white blood cell count, but they are good white blood cells. As such, we have an improved resistance to disease; we recover from injury faster and even can repair damaged organs and live longer. Remember how I was limping when we walked back to the car at the Caves."

"Yes, I asked if you needed help."

"That was a noticeable limp, by the time we got here, my limp was almost gone." Zephrin sat on a chair, taking off his shoe. "See that real nasty black and blue bruise?"

"The proverbial blind man couldn't miss it."

"It should be almost gone in the morning, along with the bruises on my arms and chest."

"Why are you stronger?"

"Yes, we're stronger, as you saw. Perhaps it's a linked trait to our anemia. But we have stronger muscle tissue. I don't know much about the physiology of it. Our muscles are a little bigger than normal and with that type of tissue, makes us stronger."

"So, what are your plans?"

"In the morning I'll call my parents and see what they know and want to do. After that, I'll get you home and then probably head home myself."

"Just so you know, Zephrin, I don't think you're lying, this time, but I'm not sure I believe you either. You lied to me about many important things. I need time to process what I've seen and what you've told me."

During the night, Brielle woke up and went to the bathroom. Then sat on the bed, her arms wrapped around her legs, her head on her knees, softly crying."

"Is everything alright, Ms. Chalmers," Gina asked. Her speaker and the laptop still on the dresser, where it was placed last night.

"Yes, Gina, I'm just having a hard time sleeping."

"You've been through, and been told, a lot."

"Yes, I…wait, you know?"

"Gina knows about Zephrin being a vampire."

"I forget, you're just a computer program, so of course you know."

"Gina is so much more than a computer program, Brielle. Gina knows that Zephrin respects you and I'm fairly sure he likes you, a lot."

"How do you know that?"

"Because, you're the second human girl that he's ever told about what he is."

"So, who was the first?"

"In 1945 there was this rather socially clumsy but rabidly attractive young man. He fell in love with a teenager, who'd come in third place in a beauty contest. They had been carrying on for a few years when he told her his secret and that, despite his unbridled passion and love for her, he couldn't stand the pain of watching his love age, so they parted. I've never seen him like this since he was with her."

"What was her name?"

"Zephrin never told Gina her name."

"But if that's true, that would mean Zephrin is over a hundred years old!"

"Yes, it would, dear."

"You mean it's all true?"

"Yes dear, it is. Think on this, as well. If vampires need to keep their existence a secret, why would Zephrin tell you instead of just killing you? Now, you go back to sleep, I've a few programs to run. It's been a surprising day for me as well."

"Okay, sleepyhead, time to wake up," said Zephrin, tossing a pillow at her as she lay in the bed.

"Hey, I didn't sleep well. I'm still a little tired."

"The couch was rather comfortable and that seems to be a standard location for me when we're together."

"Ha-ha, but after what happened yesterday, you're lucky you were still in the room."

Brielle sat up, holding the sheet around her. She saw that the bruises on his arms were a third of their size from last night and the large bruise on his ankle/leg was at about half its size. She smiled at Zephrin.

"Good morning and I'm sorry for what I said."

"No need to be, I understand. Breakfast will be here in about fifteen minutes. The shower is all yours. Some clothes will be delivered. I took the liberty of having Gina order clothes based on your size and estimated weight. Gina never told me either. After we eat, I'll be on the phone with my parents."

He left the bedroom as Brielle turned on the TV, for CNN news.

"We repeat. About forty-five minutes ago, the plane carrying the family of Jacob Asbeel Fidelus. The CEO of Doner Plastics crashed into the mountainside, about three miles from Pike's Peak. The NTSB and FAA are on route to the scene. We've no report if there are any survivors.

The family was going to Los Angeles so they could catch their flight to Hawaii, for a vacation."

Zephrin came quickly into the room, his eyes wide. "Did the report say Jacob Asbeel Fidelus?"

"Why yes, it did. Do you know him?"

"I know of him. He was a vampire and an especially important one. In America, vampires are governed by a five-member council. Jacob was one of their council."

"You don't think…"

"About that accident coupled with what happened yesterday, yes I do."

There was a knock on the door, with a voice announcing room service. Breakfast was on one cart and four boxes, one being a shoe box, were on a second cart.

"I'll eat," said Brielle "and then shower. But first a girl can never resist opening boxes with clothes and especially shoes."

She opened them and took out a full-length red dress with green trim, a matching clutch purse and high heeled shoes.

"Gina…" Zephrin said, irritably.

"Yes dear? You told Gina to order Brielle some clothes. You didn't say what clothes. I ordered her a dress. Now, she obviously needs a purse and shoes. There should be stockings and some earrings as well in one of those boxes and another with some more personal items. Like make-up. There is a call coming from your father's office in Sofia."

"Speaker please, Gina."

"Zephrin here, Dad, what's up?" he said in Bulgarian, his father responding in the same.

"Did you see the news this morning from America?"

"Watching it now, do you know anything about this?"

"Perhaps, my sources informed me that someone asked the American Vampire Council for permission to go to war, it was denied but he was on the American Vampire Council."

"Well, now that you're here, I've information about Agate. She is indeed a feral or dementia affected vampire. Now for the surprising stuff. She was taken by a new group of vampires. To help take care of her. Do you have any knowledge of another vampire group, one that has escaped everyone's notice? One that Agate might have helped start? Oh, one of its soldiers goes by the name, Lt. Colonel William Garibaldi."

Denver, Colorado

Jeremiah Daniels was surprised as he watched the news. Such a terrible accident, yet what must be, must be. He took out his cell phone and called his banker.

"Randolph, please see that $100,000 is donated to the food bank in Casper, Wyoming."

"Of course, Jerry, I'll take care of it today."

"Thanks." He then used the intercom.

"Anthony, would you see that the package you arranged last week is sent by armed and insured courier, within the hour."

"Of course, sir, will there be anything else?"

"Not for now, thank you."

Ontario, Canada

The minivan crossed over the Peace Bridge and into Ontario Province early in the morning. They were headed for Toronto and a flight back to Warsaw.

"How is Agate doing, Angela?" asked Colonel Garibaldi.

"She still shows normal and sleeping."

"I'm not sleeping, just making sure that the right people have me."

Larry smiled saying," Welcome back, Director Agate. Dr. West sends her regards and instructions. That we provide you with most anything you need."

"That's so nice of her. What I need right now is a drink, a lot stronger than a Manhattan. Then an explanation of what happened since I have no memory of anything after seeing Brielle."

The four of them spent the rest of the trip to Toronto, explaining and answering questions. When she asked about making a phone call, Colonel Garibaldi denied such for security reasons, but once we're back in Warsaw, she could call whomever she wanted.

Cincinnati, Ohio

Laurent was also checking things out with his sources. His first stop was a gun dealer and he showed him the dart he'd kept from the caves.

"Well Janos, what is it and who makes it?"

Janos examined the dart, first holding it in his hand, then under a microscope.

What we have here is a variation of a 1.25-inch tranq dart. No maker marks and that could mean it was part of a flechette round and modified or it was made that way. My guess would be the former. As for who made it, I could give you ten or twelve manufacturers, so no practical way to trace it. I will say that you might be right about what was in it. There's no way I can tell, but if I was going to make such a dart, I'd use silver nitrate and garlic in a solution."

"Why?"

"The garlic would be enough, make you drowsy or sick. The silver nitrate would cause a lot of pain and might even help speed the garlics effect. I don't think that there would be any effect on a human. This way, you have an injured but not dead comrade who you need to take care of. That means having someone take care of him. If he was out or dead, you might not be able to tell. This way, two people are now occupied, the one who was shot and the one taking care of that person. A rather smart way to win a fight without killing very many.

Cleveland, Ohio

Zephrin's mom joined the conversation, speaking in Bulgarian.

"What do you mean by another group, Zephrin?"

"When we arrived where Agate was, I encountered Laurent, Jania Mikos, and the Silas twins. Jania challenged me to a Draco Vydra duel. She's tough; we were both bloodied when two things happened. First, Agate, under the effects of dementia, attacked Laurent and me. Then a Colonel Garibaldi or an associate shot her with something that knocked her out and alleviated her feral state. They said that it was their job to rescue Agate so they can treat and take care of her, for a group she helped start. It was a three-way standoff, Laurent, with his group, Garibaldi with his and me. Agate, during her fight with Laurent and me, said that Laurent and I are half-brothers and that Talrya thought Laurent was dead, care to comment, Mom?"

Back in Sofia, Talrya's face went pale and she got dizzy, using her hand to steady herself. The baby! Agate didn't kill the baby and never told me! The baby is Laurent?

"Zephrin, four years before I married your father, I had a baby. Due to the circumstances of its birth, I didn't want it. Agate said she took care of the problem. I and your father need to make some calls, redeem some favors, and maybe remove a few arms or heads. I will find out what I can about this other group. Are you sure that they mean her no harm?"

"Yes, though I don't know why. My gut feeling is that what this Garibaldi told me was the truth."

"Good. I'll contact our ambassador to the UN. I'll see about having you listed as a diplomatic member of the Bulgarian governments embassy," Talrya said.

"Zephrin, I don't like hearing about Asbeel's death. He was one of the five American Vampire Council members, so I'll get some help for you in Cleveland. They'll be there within eighteen hours, so stay put. We'll be in contact, we love you, son."

"Love you too, Mom and Dad."

Brielle emerged from the bedroom, wearing the outfit that had been ordered for her. She walked up to Zephrin and gave him a long, lingering kiss, licking his lips with her tongue.

"About our conversation last night. I believe you, Zephrin. I don't know why, but I do, even though I'm not sure I want to. There's something about you and inside of me, that makes me feel, makes me know that you're telling the truth. A little more about me. I told you my parents died when I was seven, in a car accident but I never told you about it. I was in the car, middle of the backseat, because I liked to look out the windshield. A dump truck ran a red light making a turn and smashed into the front of our car. My parents had their heads crushed, blood and brains sprayed all over me. At the age of seven, I saw, felt, and tasted what death and blood are like. It took years of therapy for me to forget that night. The thug I killed the other night only brought back memories of that accident. Memories which I thought, I prayed, I'd been able to forget. I discovered they weren't forgotten. They'd only been buried. They resurfaced. I wanted to blame you. But how could some thugs trying to rob us be your fault? I even took a shower, early in the morning trying to 'wash' the blood, brains and gore off me. Then, things became complicated when we looked at that painting. You admitted to not telling me about Agate being your grandmother. I saw you find a piece of paper in a secret compartment of Agate's bed. I was appalled that you lied yet intrigued by what was happening. Your explanation for the lies made sense, but you were still lying.

Many guys have tried to get me into bed. That was your most endearing charm, you didn't. You treated me like a person, never used your money as a point of interest. You made me laugh and cry. You have an ability like Agate does, to make people feel comfortable with you. You talked to me, not at me. Yet, you lied and that's hard to forgive and forget. I understand, it was all in the name of doing your job and protecting your secret. You must have been in agony thinking that you'd have to kill your grandmother. Maybe, that's why I believe you. Could vampires be real? I don't know anymore. How do I tell my brother that the guy

I recently met, and that I like, is a nice guy, but he just happens to think he's a vampire?"

Ashland, Ohio

Chuck Thompkins was going over all the information that had accumulated as they re-investigated Professor d'Estange's disappearance. Everything about her record at Sorbonne checked out. Her Ashland file gave her high marks and she was well respected by her fellow students but hadn't been seen in three weeks. Word back from police in Sofia, Bulgaria had confirmed that there were no d'Estange's in Sofia. They would check the marriage records, but that would take time.

The Police Nationale, had informed them that there were many d'Estange's in France.

Zarkof's weird theory about the two men being murdered due to their rare anemic blood condition made some sense. They just couldn't find anything to support that. They discovered one highly coincidental but legally provable fact; they were related to members of the Jewish community in Helena, Montana.

The Italian embassy had confirmed Colonel Zephrin Ivano's passport, employment, civilian and military records along with his residency. Per their records, his father had died of a heart attack in 2005 and his mother had passed of Alzheimer's in 2008.

The last he knew was that Zephrin and Brielle Chalmers had left for Cleveland. He had it all put into a box, everything, and sent to Zarkof, at his request. He did keep a copy just in case someone accidentally deleted something.

Marie Currie Institute, Warsaw, Poland

Dr. Maven West was going over Agate d'Estange's blood test.

"Marie, please log the following into Agate's medical record. Test dose #11 has been effective for 7 hours and 18 minutes. Recent blood work shows that it will wear off in another two to three hours. I will enter the room and talk with her."

"Recorded, Dr. West, would you like me to keep recording your conversation with Agate?"

"Yes."

Maven walked down the hall and knocked at a door.

"Come in."

"Good afternoon, Agate, how's everything going?"

"I haven't felt the craving for at least six hours Sorry about the dent I put in my door last night. I will say, my last injection didn't make me sick. I've eaten two meals today. How much longer do I have?"

"About two and a half hours, plus or minus some."

"Well at least it isn't getting any shorter. My deepest thanks for being able to reach me before the others did, I'd like to make a phone call, please."

"I don't see why not, though we'd have Marie monitor all calls, just in case. Who are you going to call, Zephrin?"

"Maybe, but first a very special unexpected complication, that's who."

Maven took out her phone. "Use mine. Marie, please monitor the line and the call for security purposes only."

"Security systems are active, Dr. West," replied Marie

She handed the phone to Agate.

"Talk as long as you want. When done, Marie will let me know."

"Thank you, Maven, this means a lot to me."

"No problem, what else was I supposed to do? My older sister asked for my help. It's a six-hour difference between here and Ohio."

Maven left and Agate dialed a number.

Back in Cleveland, Zephrin and Brielle were having a very romantic interlude, kissing on the couch after a day of shopping. Several items purchased were being sent to Brielle's home. They heard the ringing of a telephone.

"If it was mine, Gina would've told me."

Brielle kissed Zephrin, slowly getting off the couch they were sharing, their hands lingering, as she took her phone from her purse and walked into the bedroom. She didn't recognize the number.

"Hello?"

"Why dear, this is Agate. How are you doing and where are you?"

"Agate! Where the hell are you? Did you escape? Just what the hell is going on?"

"Relax, Brielle. I won't tell you where I am but I'm doing better and I've no need to escape. Again, how are you doing and where are you?"

"Fine, I guess. I'm at a hotel in Cleveland."

"Is my grandson with you?"

"Yes, but I'm in the bedroom and he was on the couch when I left him."

"I know you saw everything. I'm sorry about that and for never telling you but I really couldn't, now could I? How much did he tell you about us?"

"I understand, sort of, and he told me the best that he could about anemia, muscles and such."

"He never did like science; I'd box his ears right now if I could. Do you believe?"

"I think so, yes, but I don't really know why."

"I'll be sending my resignation in to the University, medical reasons. Sorry to put you through all this. I don't know if you and Zephrin have anything going on, but I need to tell you that you are special, Brielle, incredibly special. I'd like you to stay with Zephrin, for several reasons, especially now that Laurent is involved. It would be nice if you did. Either way, I'll recommend that you take over the department, that's, if you want to. Don't answer; you probably don't have one yet. All isn't over, yet I've no advice to give you, except Zephy will protect you. Have you unwrapped my painting for you gaining tenure?"

"Yes, and I was very surprised, to say the least."

"The painting, as you've probably figured out, is more than just a painting. Remember that a painting is just temporary. Like bad memories it fades with time and the tears it creates. Keep flowers my dear, you've always looked good with flowers."

"Can I call you if I need to?"

"You call this number and maybe I'll be able to talk. Rest assured I'm safe and happy and I really do wish you the same."

"Thank you, Agate."

"You're welcome, dear." The call ended and Brielle went back into the room and sat down next to Zephrin.

"That is a most interesting look on your face. Was that bad news?"

"No, but it was fascinating. Maybe, if you need to know, I'll tell you about it."

"Touché Brielle, well then, would you like to catch dinner out, a movie, or shopping? It will be awhile until my parents call back."

"We'll do some shopping in Ashland tomorrow, and its nothing like we did yesterday in Cleveland." Brielle looked at Zephrin, a sensual smile forming on her face. She tilted her head, raised her eyebrows, running her tongue across her lips, barely parting them.

"You've caught a minx, Zephrin. What have I caught?" as she slowly inched closer. She felt Zephrin's hair rise as her arms wrapped around his neck. Her soft lips, grazing across his forehead, produced an expectant moan from Zephrin. Like a vixen, Brielle curled up in Zephrin's lap. Through the soft silk of her dress, she felt her breasts bury themselves in Zephrin's chest. They were locked in a sensual bout of kissing. With the utmost of control, Brielle backed off, pulling her head barely away from Zephrin. She ran her tongue across the roof of his mouth, and quickly around his lips. This evoked more pleasurable gasps from Zephrin. She backed away just enough so that her lips pulled on his lower lip, sucking it, and flicking it with her tongue. Zephrin responded by sucking her upper lip and squeezing her breasts as he sat up. Brielle was still sitting on Zephrin's lap as he tore the dress in half, tossing the pieces aside. Brielle did the same to Zephrin's shirt, buttons flying, which ended up keeping the torn dress and shirt company on the floor. Brielle resumed her assault, kissing Zephrin on his left ear. Trolling her moist tongue around the ear lobe then flicking it, before lightly blowing in his ear. She felt the heat of his passion as she teasingly traversed down his neck, giving it light bites, brief tongue licks and kisses. Zephrin's hand was twisting and pulling on Brielle's hard nipple, her gasps of pleasure on his neck, matched the warmth between her legs.

He whispered in her ear "So, who's the vampire now?" as he licked the outside of her ear. Then he sucked in air, over the area he had just licked. He hummed while kissing her ear lobe. Brielle responding with a whispered "feels great."

"Let's move to your bedroom, dear."

"Zephy, what took you so long to ask?"

"My mind was occupied by a very beautiful and seductive lady, sitting on my lap."

Zephrin carried her to the bedroom, while kissing her passionately. Their loving lasted a couple of hours. They lay facing each other, softly caressing and smiling.

 "For an older man, that wasn't bad," Brielle said as she dragged her tongue across his lips. "You did say you were 117 years old."

"Old, am I? I'm curious, what is the age limit for vixens in Ohio? Twenty-five, I hope. I'd hate to find out that you aren't a keeper or that I was hunting without a license." He reached his hand to envelope her breast.

Brielle used her arm to prop her head up and allowing Zephrin's hand a little more room, while staring at Zephrin.

"Okay, your smile is as big as the sun and you're glowing, what's on your mind?"

"You have very seductive and sexy eyes. I thought they were hazel but they're actually green."

"Both our eyes are like that," Zephrin replied, as he pulled her to him.

He kissed her then his tongue searched hers out. She sighed, her tongue joining his in a sexy and seductive dance. Her hand began moving down his body, like a spider. It stopped between his legs, she caressed him with her fingertips.

 Brielle, whispered, "I'm a keeper, old man, and this vixen is very protective of what she values." She kissed her way down his chest, using her hands to give slight pulls on his chest hair. Her kissing ending at the intended destination. She teased and tantalized him, enjoying the musical sounds of his pleasure.

 "That feels utterly fantastic!"

She moved on top, taking Zephrin inside of her. It felt so good, she had goosebumps. They both enjoyed the second session, then fell asleep in each other's arms. In the morning, Zephrin let Brielle have the shower but made sure she ordered some clothes from a nearby store, to be delivered within the hour. He was cleaning up when Gina appeared on the wall.

"My, my, that's the second time you've ripped that dress. Don't you like red and green?"

"It's the second time I've been in love with who was wearing it, Gina."

"Yes, but are you doing it with all parts of your heart this time, dear? There are many who don't get even one chance at love, you have a second. 'Non rovinare tutto' or, in English-Don't fuck it up."

"Gina, it's the same as with you, we'll both suffer as she grows old and I don't."

"Zephrin, you are a selfish jerk! Brielle cares for you and you her, do the both of you a favor and grow up."

She came from the bedroom, wearing a sweater and jeans; her hair was in a bun at the back of her head. She looked at Zephrin in his slacks and formal shirt. Zephrin handed her a cup of coffee he'd made.

"Dear, we've got to get you some slumming clothes, jeans, sneakers, polo shirts. You look nice but you stick out. Maybe some bling to accessorize," she responded as they mutually kissed each other.

They sat for breakfast as they talked.

"So, making me more presentable, I see."

"You've got formal nailed, but casual, maybe in Venice but not here, that's all. We'll take care of that in Ashland."

"Speaking of Venice, do you have a passport?"

"No, why do you ask?"

"We may be traveling between Venice and the states a few times."

"What if I want to stay?" asked Brielle as she stopped eating and stared at Zephrin.

"I'm fairly sure that Agate won't be back. I can live there, until what's going on with Laurent sorts itself out. You're welcome to stay at Agate's old house, as often as you like."

Brielle spilled her coffee when she heard that. "One exquisite night with you and your asking me to move in? I'm flattered and I just might accept, down the road. Let's see how we do for a while before I answer. How will you do your business from Ashland?"

"I'm tied into the business with Gina, so between phone and computer, I should be fine. Besides, I own the company, maybe being a CEO type isn't that bad. I can have any changes or set-up I need put in at Agate's house."

Brielle walked over and sat in Zephrin's lap and kissed him lightly.

"That phone call I got last night was Agate. She said she's doing fine and is safe. She wouldn't tell me where she is. She's not coming back to Ashland and said she'd see that I got her position if I wanted it. She mentioned the painting she gave me. We should check that painting out again. She said something about me looking better around flowers. By the way, is your living in her Ashland home something you feel is best for me or best for you? I ask because, either way, I'm involved in that decision and it's so different than ordering food for me to eat."

"Last week, I'd have given you a different answer but today, I think it's best for both of us. I care about you, Brielle, and as you can guess, that's hard for me. I want to be with you and for us to learn more about each other."

"That's good to hear," as she kissed him while getting off his lap.

"Now, let's get me, us, on the road. The day is nice and since you made us food, and I ate all of it, I will buy you clothes that you'll wear."

Cincinnati, Ohio

Laurent Fortesque was shocked as he was watching the news. Dr. Daniels, you surprisingly idiotic genius!

He called Jania Mikos.

"So, Jania, feeling better?"

"Yes, so how did your meeting with the cave wall go?"

"It made an impression that few others have. How does using a straw to drink your food feel? Okay, events didn't transpire as I expected. You saw the news this morning?"

"Yes, your point?"

"That just changed the rules of the game. However, I need you to investigate this other group. You've more knowledge about what my newly discovered grandmother is like, so find this group she helped start and get me everything you can. We have one name, Lt. Colonel William Garibaldi, and something about Zephrin's computer. I'm not concerned about time or expense, just find them. How did you find Agate?"

"That picture of the map you gave me was the key. It took a while, but they weren't travel markers, well if so, well-chosen ones. Sure, it'll be hard, but no group can remain secret, money always leaves a trail."

"Yes, and I'm counting on that. If you need other technical specialists, I'll get them for you. But I repeat NO actions beyond investigative are to be taken. Things will be changing quickly, yet I don't want you distracted from finding this other group."

Well, I've more pressing matters right now. Like what is my new half-brother doing?

Laurent went back to thinking about what Agate had said. That he and Zephrin were half-brothers, two ways for that, same father, or same mother. Since Agate had said it, he'd go with mother, yet Talrya had never contacted him about it and that's not the vampire way. You might be the black sheep of the family, but you were still family. Agate mentioned sins to atone for, what sins? She's not my mother; she'd be my grandmother, which means that my mother sent me away. Why? Was she married and she had a lover or was she single and didn't want me around? Again, that's not our way, if the child is acknowledged by one of the parents, so what are Agate's sins, unless she wasn't supposed to give me away but bury me?"

Ashland, Ohio

Gina's voice was heard. "Your father is calling back, Zephrin."

Zephrin and Brielle were lying on the couch. They untangled from each other's arms.

"Gina, despite being a computer, you're timing always seems to be bad," Zephrin chided.

"Gina is a caring person, not an unemotional computer entity, which is what you wanted. Brielle, I see you've got some clothes. Sorry about the dress, I ordered another one for you. Zephrin, would you like video or just audio?"

"Okay Gina, put my father on speaker please."

"Yes, Dad, how's Mom?"

"I'm fine dear," his mom replied. "I need to find the best way to explain, at least better than I already did."

"So, what Agate said was true?"

"Yes, but I didn't know it until I heard what you said. Several years before I met your father, I was raped by my uncle, Armin Vambery. Agate delivered the baby and I demanded that she kill it. She told me that she took care of the problem. So, yes, Laurent is your half-brother that I never knew survived more than six hours after birth. Your father never knew until I explained, after I had recovered from the shock of what you told me."

"Well, Mom, nothing much any of us can do about it. My half-brother wants to kill me, and the feeling is mutual, I assure you. It would be an ironic twist of fate if the rest of the vampire world knew this. You need to see what you can find about this group that took Agate to care for her and prevent both me and Laurent from getting her."

"Actually Zephrin, we have something more important. You know about the plane crash and that someone in America asked the American Vampire Council for permission to go to war and kill you. It was refused and I think that this is the result of the denial. I think that the remaining American Vampire Council member's lives might be at risk. A second vampire civil war might start very soon. You should consider yourself in a war zone. When does your flight home leave?"

"Seven O'clock tonight but I'm staying in Ashland. I think Agate might have left some clues behind and I need to check them out. I think Ashland will be a relatively safe location for now."

"Can you delay until the help your father is sending gets there?"

"I could, but don't send any help, Dad. Mom, one thing I want you to consider."

"What is it, dear?"

"Call and talk to Laurent."

About the Author

Jeffrey was born in Corning, New York and now braves the winters of the Rochester, NY area. Jeffrey is married with three children and a Pomeranian that was there one night when he got home. He spent a few years teaching History and later earned an MS that helps him with his current managerial job.

Jeff has had several stories published. *Unexpected Opportunity* (February 2015, Aphelion), *Dandelion Dreams* (Flash Fiction Press 11-23-2015), *Umbrae Calling* (Flash Fiction Press 1-25-2016) *Their Very First Battle* (Flash Fiction Press 1-31-2017), poem: *To Meet Others* (The Question of the Day: The Andre Polk Memorial Anthology, Clayborn Press, 9-2017)

He enjoys reading, science fiction, fantasy, and historical genres. It was his enjoyment of history and the question, how did the myth of vampires originate, that led him to write the book; *SUNDOWNERS: Vampires are Only Human.*

www.ingramcontent.com/pod-product-compliance
Lightning Source LLC
Chambersburg PA
CBHW072229170626
46813CB00003B/1146